MW00587876

BIG WORLD

BIG WORLD

STORIES BY MARY MILLER

Short Flight / Long Drive Books
a division of HOBART

SHORT FLIGHT / LONG DRIVE BOOKS
a division of HOBART
PO Box 1658
Ann Arbor, MI 48106
www.hobartpulp.com/minibooks

Copyright © 2009 by Mary Miller
Introduction copyright © 2010 by Chris Offutt

The following stories have appeared elsewhere,
some in slightly different format:

"Leak," in *Oxford American*, reprinted in *New Stories from the South, 2008*; "Even the Interstate is Pretty," in *Mississippi Review*; "Pearl" in *Hobart*; "Aunt Jemima's Old Fashioned Pancakes" in *Barrelhouse*; "My Brother in Christ" as "Go Fish" in *Barrelhouse* online; "Full" in *Mississippi Review* online; "Cedars of Lebanon" in *The Collagist*.

Library of Congress Control Number: 2008942939

ISBN: 978-0-9749541-8-9

Printed in the United States of America

Second Edition

Inside text set in Georgia
Front and back cover paintings by David Kramer

for my family

I wanted it to be harder. I wanted my photo taken. These would be my dominant reactions to many situations for the rest of my life.
    Heather Sellers

TABLE OF CONTENTS

INTRODUCTION

– CHRIS OFFUTT, 2010

Like most people who write short fiction, I read a great many story collections. There is nothing quite like recognizing high quality prose by an unknown writer. It's a kind of private ecstasy, as if I have made the discovery myself, alone in my favorite reading chair, carried away by the imaginary worlds of each story. The sensation of this occurs very rarely.

Mary Miller is that most uncommon occurrence in literature—a natural writer in possession of narrative confidence, a bold precision of language, and a willingness to take great risks with story, structure, and character.

I came upon her work in one of the many literary quarterlies that arrive in the mail, and after reading her story I immediately ordered *Big World*. It's a physically small book, which made me think I'd zip through it in a day and move on to the next one on my pile. Instead, I read one or two stories per day over the course of a week. I savored them, captivated by the power and directness of her voice, entranced by the jolt of insight and understanding. A lovely and brittle lyricism in the sentences often leads to stunning shifts—a detail snaps an image in place, or an apparently off-hand comment abruptly sharpens the character to a three-dimensional living human being.

Often, as I read, I found myself wondering in the back of my head how she'd manage to end the story, to get out of the world. Each time I was surprised.

After finishing the book, I read it again, swiftly this time, endeavoring to see if they really were as good as I thought. I was gratified to realize they were better on a second reading; the entire book was. Though two generations and a gender separate me from the narrators of these stories , I recognized elements of myself—always the mark of Literature.

My next step was to order several more copies and begin giving them to writers I knew would appreciate the work. Each person expressed an enthusiasm similar to mine. I envy any reader opening its pages for the first time. Please do yourself a favor. Quit wasting your time reading this, and get to what matters.

You will not forget these stories.

You will close the book with respect for Mary Miller.

CEDARS OF LEBANON

They had just been to IHOP, where they'd sat in the middle of the room at a two-top a couple of inches from a four-top, a man and a woman. The woman kept saying the man's name over and over again, viciously. It was a good name for hurling. They had gone in happy.

Now they were in her apartment and she was wondering how she would feel if she told him to never come back.

"I want you to say you'll take care of me," she said.

"Well I need someone to take care of me, too," he said.

He squeezed the different parts of her, saying, "These are mine, and this is mine, and this." He just loved her too much, he explained. She got up to make tea. He wanted her to help him clean out his camper so they could take it to Cedars of Lebanon. The camper was his most recent purchase, a little shit-can that said KNOCK THREE TIME HERE in sticker letters by the door. It looked like a child had put them on.

"Follow me to my house," he said, "and I'll put gas in your car." His house was in Shelbyville, home of the Tennessee Walking Horse. It was a terrible town full of friendly church-going people where she had been stopped twice for speeding. She packed some clothes into a bag and locked the door to her apartment, followed him down the steps and then to an out-of-the-way gas station where he had a card that entitled him to a ten-cent discount.

At his house, she changed clothes and went out to the camper, which he had bought as-is for three hundred dollars, the amount of money the woman who was living in it owed in rent. The air-conditioning unit alone was worth that, he'd said.

She stepped in and then stepped right back out.

"I can't believe someone actually lived here. She must have been on drugs. She must have been bad on drugs." She recognized *bad on drugs* as a saying of her father's.

He brought her a bucket of cleaning supplies: bleach and paper towels, a broom, trash bags, and a pair of gloves, and she started cleaning. She gagged and had to step outside every few minutes to get air. She wondered what she was doing, cleaning up foreign shit and piss for him. She hated doing the things he wanted her to do and he hated doing the things she wanted him to do. Because of this, they pushed each other harder.

She had even stared cooking bacon, the grease popping and burning her arms.

He hauled the mattress out and beat it with the broom while she sat on the low brick wall, drinking a glass of Kool-Aid. He declared it still good. She thought about going to Cedars of Lebanon with him and having sex on that mattress, the trashy little camper rocking. Then she thought of the piece of her cervix the doctor had removed, how he had been at work that day and couldn't go with her.

That night, he'd come over with take-out sushi and a bouquet of flowers, and she hadn't cared much for either, but she cared about the money he had spent and how it had pained him to spend it.

"Will you take me to the drive-in tonight?" she asked.

"Okay," he said.

"Can we pick up a pizza?"

"Okay," he said, smacking the mattress again.

She always fell asleep before the double feature began, but falling asleep on his chest on the wide leather seats of his old car made her feel happy and safe. She liked everything about the drive-in: the stuffed bear by the door of the snack shop, the popcorn machines and rotating hotdogs, the people in their cars doing things just so they could feel like they were getting away with something. She even liked walking half-asleep through the gravel to use the bathroom.

"I want to have it ready by next weekend," he said, opening the rest of the windows, which pushed out like the windows in old schoolhouses. She opened the door to the tiny bathroom, feeling enormous, and sprayed bleach on the walls, the sink, the toilet.

He went through the cabinets to see what the woman had left behind—a can of artichoke hearts, a cracked bar of soap, an empty carton of cigarettes—lined them up on the counter where she had probably made her sandwiches. Then he opened the refrigerator and removed an empty bottle of vodka and a jar of pickles. She threw the stuff in a garbage bag and went back to the bathroom and sprayed more bleach. She thought about the drug addict shows she liked to watch on television, how they sold their bodies, how they had run out of veins for shooting. She was glad she wasn't a drug addict.

After a few hours of this, she said she was finished and went inside and got in the shower. He got in with her and they soaped each other up and washed each other's hair. He was the only man she'd ever been with who liked to shower with her, who didn't think taking turns under the water was too much trouble.

When they were clean and dressed, their wet hair brushed back, she opened a can of beer and drank it while sitting in the middle of his king-sized bed.

"Play me 'Highwayman,'" she said, bouncing up and down. He was tired of playing "Highwayman" but he sat at the piano and played it anyway. She closed her eyes, imagining herself a sailor and a dam builder and a single drop of rain, listening to his voice strain with feeling. She would die but she would not be gone—she liked the idea of this. When he was almost finished and she was thinking about asking him to play it again, there was a knock at the door. He froze, his hands above the keys. "It's Coach," she said, falling back, the can on her stomach. Other than his tenants, Coach was the only person who ever came over unannounced.

Coach was an alcoholic P.E. instructor, a former baseball player who had maintained an array of near-debilitating superstitions: he wore certain clothes on certain days; he was always looking for wood to knock on; he had a fear of red cigarette lighters. She had once seen him take a stranger's red cigarette lighter off a table and throw it as far as he could.

She listened to them talk in booming voices. Then he came back and closed the door, opened his closet and took the brick of marijuana from his safe. She liked how careful he was, pinching it between his fingers, measuring it on the scale. She liked the way it came packaged tightly in a cellophaned slab, and she liked how he carried it in his fake leather motorcycle jacket that said U.S.A. on the back of it when he made his runs to Murfreesboro. But she didn't smoke his pot or ride on his motorcycle. She wanted to do these things but then she couldn't tell him not to do them.

"Are we still going to the drive-in?" she asked.

"I'm going to smoke with Coach first," he said.

He closed the door behind him and she laid there and thought about his ex-girlfriend, who was pregnant. She had recently seen a picture of this ex-girlfriend, at his parents' house, on the mantel, and been surprised to find her small, with flat brown hair and round glasses. She had imagined her tall and thin, swooping around his kitchen with her long hair swinging, fucked up on pills but still able to prepare a delicious meal that conformed to his Atkins diet, clean the kitchen, and pack his lunch for the next day. She thought about his ex sending him the ultrasound picture, sad it wasn't his baby, and then she went back to worrying about her weight, which went up and down and up and down, and her skin, which was broken out along the jaw line. She had this little machine that had a hot tip and she'd hold it to her pimples and it would beep every thirty seconds and her boyfriend would ask if she was playing video games in there.

She went out to the garage and sat on the steps, surrounded by a mountain of stuff he said he'd get rid of if she moved in, but she couldn't see herself living in his house. It was too much his. She thought of the shards of glass in her palms when she did pushups in the morning, the thin green carpet and broken chairs. There was nothing he was willing to change in order to have her. She lit a cigarette and stood in the driveway, looking in the kitchen window of the middle unit where the man in the wheelchair lived. She would never see his face in that window, looking back at her. Next to him, there was a new tenant named Mr. Skeet. Mr. Skeet had a truck that didn't run so she couldn't tell when he was there or not. The girl who'd lived there before had tried to fuck her boyfriend so she could move into the main house but he'd refused and she'd moved out, leaving nail polish on the linoleum and glitter ground into the carpet, fruit flies swirling up from the drains.

She sat at the table where he made his bowls and vases and figurines. On their first date, he'd made her a horse out of two thin glass pipes. Now she had a whole army of clowns and snowmen and unicorns and dogs that all had googly, mismatched eyes. She kept them in a wooden box and moved it around her apartment so she could hear them knocking into each other.

The screen door slammed and the boys came out.

"How much did you pay for this piece of shit?" Coach asked, banging his fist on the sign.

"Three hundred," her boyfriend said. "The air-conditioning unit alone is worth that."

"I don't think it'll ever air out," she said. "Smell it—smell how terrible it is."

Coach opened the door and stuck his head inside. "Jesus," he said. "That's horrible. So you're going to hook this thing up to the Lincoln?"

"He has a gun in the glove compartment," she said. He thinks it's a truck, she meant. He takes it off-roading and hops curbs. Her boyfriend looked at her and she went inside and poured a shot of Canadian Club. She stared at the glass, thinking of all the time she'd spent lying in his bed watching movies she'd already seen—all those wasted days, all the wasted days to come. She drank it and took another beer from the drawer and went back to the bedroom, leaned against the headboard with her legs under the covers.

After a while, she heard footsteps and then he was standing there in his oversized Bulls t-shirt and plaid pajama pants.

"We're going to have to move if we want to make it," he said.

She got up and helped him pack a cooler with beer and Diet Rite, grabbed a blanket and pillow off the bed while he filled his flask. Then they put everything in the car and drove the few blocks to Papa John's.

He backed into a parking spot, left the car running while he went inside to get the pizza. She didn't have to ask what kind because they always ordered the same kind: wheat crust with sausage, bacon, and pepperoni. She liked how they had things that were theirs, even if they'd been his first and she'd only adopted them. But then she found herself wondering if his ex liked wheat crust pizza and camping and Johnny Cash. If she did, it was weird and she didn't like that. If she didn't, she was jealous that the small, mousy girl had a personality that couldn't be scratched out and written over.

She wondered if he called her his June, if she had been his June first.

He put the pizza on the backseat and then opened the front door and stuck a leg in. She looked at his leg, the rip in his pajama pants, and then at his mouth, which was shouting across the parking lot to one of his students. Everywhere they went, they saw his students and his students' parents and he had to pretend like he wasn't a pot-smoking hippie despite his long hair and hand-me-down vehicles, the one-hitter tucked into his underwear. And somehow, impossibly, he made it work, which made her hate people. It also made her hate her boyfriend but she hated everyone else more because her boyfriend knew what a fake he was; he accepted it as the way things had to be in order to get what he wanted.

The double feature always showed a new release with an older movie. Tonight it was *Final Destination 3* and *Caddyshack*. She was excited about *Final Destination 3*. He had the other two on DVD and they'd watched them together and now they were going to see the third. And if a fourth one came out, they'd see that, too.

He put the car in park, his lights shining on the screen a moment before he cut them, and then turned the radio up so the opening music filled the car. She slipped her flip flops off and put her feet on the dash. She had just painted her toenails the color of pink sand and they looked good, like porn stars with their tan breasts, the nipples just a shade darker. She wiggled her toes, hoping he might say they looked pretty, that he might take one of her feet in his hands and hold it in his palm. He reached into the backseat for the paper towels and tore off two. Already she had to pee.

"I have to pee," she said. She looked at him, as if waiting for him to say it was okay, and rubbed the thin material of his pants between her fingers. Why did she have to love him more than he loved her? She wanted him to be the one turning over in his sleep to feel for her, making sure she was still there.

"Well, hurry up," he said.

Her flip flops crunched as she walked over the gravel. She looked inside the cars and trucks, the couple who'd brought camping chairs and sat outside. These people didn't have to get drunk or high, and the man would not, at some point, unzip his pants and press the woman's head to his crotch, hold it there until he was done.

The man caught her eye as he took a bite of his hot dog. She looked away and then felt the woman's eyes follow her.

She greeted the bear with its bag of plastic yellow popcorn, its mouth open in a kind of benevolent smile, and shoved the door open, glancing at the old man bent over the counter.

The place was large and clean and brightly-lit, the bathroom stalls designed for people with special needs and small children. While she peed, she tried to think of things she was interested in, wondering if she could make him like some of the things she liked. She liked tennis, but she didn't have access to a court. She hardly ever finished a book anymore. She hadn't played chess in years. She washed her hands and then stood in the mirror and looked at her eyes, which were big and dark and lost—a good look, really—and realized that all of the things she liked or did were things she didn't like or do any more, were things no one would associate with her.

She woke up hungover in his big bed alone—the memory of water running, his lips on her forehead. She thought about driving the hour back to her apartment, which was in a part of Nashville that was full of tire stores and ethnic groceries and gas stations that wouldn't take her debit card unless she spent ten dollars. Instead, she drank a Diet Rite while sitting on his kitchen counter, kicking her legs. She took her bottle of weight control multivitamins from the windowsill and opened the childproof cap, swallowed one with her soda. Then she looked at her belly button, an innie so deep she couldn't see the bottom of it.

She jumped off the counter and gathered her things, locked the door behind her.

As she backed out of the driveway, she looked in the wheelchair man's window, a small dark square. She wondered what he did all day, how he occupied his time well enough so he didn't have to shoot himself in the head. Sometimes she'd talk to him when he was sunning himself in the drive-way, his thin but otherwise normal-looking legs exposed, and she'd ask him invasive questions and then apologize and he'd say it was okay but he would never give her any answers.

There was no welcome mat in front of her door, no inflatable rafts on her balcony. If she got too comfortable, if her neighbors could recognize her by her birdfeeders and windchimes and beach towels, she thought she might remain there forever.

On the balcony, there were two discolored plastic chairs. One of them was cracked and pinched her legs. She sat in the other and watched the guy she called the serial killer walk down the hill with his poodle. The poodle stopped and cen-tered its body and barked at her as she lit a ciga-rette. The man was homeless-thin with a goatee and eyes that couldn't look at her straight on. It was fucked up, eyes like that. The serial killer had once stood at her balcony and asked if he could come up and she'd said no, she had a boyfriend. The maintenance man said he wasn't a serial killer at all but a mild retard who lived with his parents and was licensed to carry a gun.

She called her sister and then went back inside and sat on the couch, put her feet on the coffee table. Her coffee table held an array of picture books, like other people's coffee tables: Delta blues joints and modern-day Prague and famous models, things she had no interest in whatsoever. Young Lauren Hutton with that gap between her teeth, Kate Moss looking sexily abused against a faux-wood wall.

After a while, there was a tentative knock at the door, a knock too light to belong to her sister. She looked out the peephole and then opened it to an enormous sweat-streaked girl. The girl said she was in this class and had to develop her social skills by talking to strangers. She was suspicious so she asked the girl what she was selling but she insisted she wasn't selling anything so she invited her in and gave her a glass of water. The girl flattered her, saying that nobody else had given her a glass of water, nobody else had let her sit on their couch, and after five minutes the girl handed her a form with little boxes for her name and address. She said she didn't want any magazines and the girl got angry. The girl said if she didn't buy some magazines, she wouldn't get to go to Europe and her life would probably be ruined.

She shut the door and locked it and then went back to the bathroom to see if her swimsuit was dry. It was still damp but she put it on anyway and shaved her bikini line while imagining the fat girl wandering through museums and taking pictures of things she'd seen in her guidebook, trying to replicate them exactly. When she'd gone to France, she'd had difficulty with the toilets—there was either a pedal on the floor or a string hanging from the ceiling or a button somewhere and you had to figure it out. One time, she couldn't figure it out and had had to leave her shit floating in the bowl. Who wanted to go to Europe? And everything was too small and the women were too thin. The girl wouldn't have liked it there.

Her sister arrived wearing a pink trucker hat and a pair of cut-off overalls. She was a songwriter who wrote in the mornings so they'd spend their afternoons laying out or going to bars. Other days, they'd meet at a coffee shop and jot down bits of overheard conversation in the hopes that there might be a song somewhere, but then they'd just talk about how every song had already been written a million times.

"Do you want some brie?" she asked, standing in front of the refrigerator. She tore off a hunk and put it in her mouth.

"I can't eat brie," her sister said.

"I thought you could eat whatever you wanted."

"I can but I only get twenty-three points a day and I've already used fourteen. Plus, I want to drink later and that's going to mess everything up."

"That sucks," she said.

Her sister told her about the extra weekly points that were optional, for the all-or-nothing people who freaked out and ate a bucket of fried chicken and then said *fuck it*.

She put a towel in a bag, a book and a bottle of sunscreen, and they walked up the hill to the pool. They claimed a couple of chairs and pointed them at the sun.

"Can you hear me swallow?" her sister asked, taking a sip of Diet Coke. "I don't like it when people can hear me swallow." She took another swig and laid a stack of magazines between them, fall fashion issues. They flipped through the shiny pages—the annoying sales pitches flying out, the smell of perfume—looking at the boots and jackets, folding down corners. It was ninety degrees.

They read their horoscopes but they were next month's horoscopes, completely irrelevant.

"Look at this girl's eyes," her sister said. "What's wrong with her face?" She turned the magazine sideways. "Her face isn't symmetrical at all."

"I think it's the camera angle."

"No—look how small this eye is. It's like that in both pictures. This girl is ugly."

She walked over to the ladder and jumped

in, swam down to the bottom and felt along the scratchy concrete, the water sort of cloudy. When she came up, a thick boy was clobbering past. She swallowed some water and paddled over to the side, her sister laughing.

After a few hours, they walked back down the hill to her apartment to look for something to eat. They each had a cup of blueberries: one point. Then she changed clothes and followed her sister to her condo downtown, which was across the street from the trashy karaoke bar where they sometimes ended up late at night, drinking whiskey until close; next to the sushi bar where the man charged whatever he wanted and refused to serve tourists. From her condo, they could walk to Mojo's or the Beer Cellar or any of the bars along Broadway that had musicians playing at three o'clock on a weekday.

Her boyfriend called while they were sitting outside a Mexican restaurant they'd wandered into. They were drinking Corona Light while looking over the big plastic menus, her sister slurping salsa off a chip until it was too soggy to do anything but swallow it.

"Are you coming back over?" he asked.

"I want to but I've been drinking," she said.

"I want to see you. I want to spend some

quality time with you."

"I want to see you, too." She'd only left because she wanted him to miss her. She wanted him to see that she had things to do: she had jobs to apply for and a sister who needed her. She could go out and buy things like plants and groceries and then she'd have to water the plants so they wouldn't die and cook the food so it wouldn't go bad.

"Your boyfriend is a drug-dealing scumbag," her sister said, after she'd hung up.

"He only sells to the people who'd smoke his pot anyway," she said, knowing how ridiculous it sounded. It was like the time she'd dated the Nazi—she had made excuses because she was already in love with him by the time he put on his Nazi officer's jacket and pointed a gun at a black man carrying groceries. He was drunk. The gun hadn't been loaded. He was under a lot of pressure at work.

She didn't want another relationship to fail, didn't know if she'd be able to try again. She had sex with a man and then fell in love with him, and when he turned out to be all wrong, it seemed like there was nothing to do but try and make it work anyway. She had done this with her ex-husband for six years before leaving.

She put her phone on silent and they had a conversation about which one of them was the most delicate. They both wanted to be the most delicate sister—the most delicate meant they were the most special, it meant they needed love and attention beyond what was normally given.

The next day, she drove back to Shelbyville and hung around her boyfriend's house while he was at work. She did sets of twenty push-ups and watched television and looked at the glasswork lining his walls—little men perched on the vases and bowls, fishing or just dangling their legs, their bodies pieced together like children's toys. She had never seen such ugly work, wanted to snap off their arms and legs. Years ago, he'd just been a glassblower living out of a van, a college drop-out. She thought they might have been a better fit then, when he was who he said he was.

He called and said he was coming home for lunch so she looked in the refrigerator for something to fix. There was mayonnaise and milk and butter and wheat tortillas and ground beef, the usual things she didn't know how to put together to add up to a meal, so she fixed what she normally fixed: eggs and bacon and cheese on a piece of wheat toast with sugar-free jelly. By the time he unlocked the door, she had it ready on a plate with a glass of Kool-Aid.

She sat next to him while he ate and listened

to the wheelchair man roll around, flush his toilet.

"How's your day going so far?" she asked.

The way he described it, his job was to flirt with the women who worked in the office and keep the teachers in line, which also typically required flirting. Sometimes he paddled kids. She liked to ask about the teachers, if any of them were pretty, if he wanted to fuck them. He only claimed to like one and she was married and had a kid.

"Have you worked on the camper any more?" he asked, spreading jelly onto an egg. "I was thinking we could take it out this weekend. I'll put the TV and DVD player in there and we'll watch movies and blast the A/C."

It was exactly what they did at home. "It smells bad," she said.

"It's airing out. I bet it smells better already."

They went outside to the trailer, and she stood there while he pointed out what still needed to be done: the dead bugs cleared from the windowsills, the inside of the refrigerator wiped down. He opened the door to the bathroom and they looked at the sludge that had collected at the drain. She thought about the woman again and how she had shit and showered and shot up all in that tiny space.

"I'll throw up if I have to sleep in here," she

said, but she kind of liked the idea of it. She thought about watching something hopelessly depressing like *21 Grams* or *The Basketball Diaries* while he filled the trailer with pot smoke. And later, he'd grill hotdogs and they'd eat them on paper plates, and if she asked how old they were, or how many times they'd thawed and been refrozen, he'd tell her that hot dogs never went bad, that they were like space food, like MREs. And then she'd get on her knees and suck him off and maybe he'd leave her a few dollars, like he did sometimes, so she could take herself out to lunch.

She wiped down the refrigerator and the cabinets, the counter once again for good measure, scooped the bugs out of the windows. There were a lot of bugs, their stiff wings crumbling. When she was finished, she sat outside on the wall and took off her shirt, wearing only a pair of shorts and a sports bra. When she'd been 125 pounds, she'd told herself that she could exercise in her sports bra at 120 pounds, but then she'd still been too fat so she'd set a new goal. But now that she was finally skinny enough, she realized what a stupid goal it had been, to exercise in public wearing as little as possible. She was uncomfortable even now, though she knew what she was doing, waiting for the wheelchair man to come out, wanting him to see her. She pictured the two of them swimming in the lake, bobbing together in the brown water, how he would be like everyone else then. How she'd wrap her legs around him and squeeze him so tight and he wouldn't know the difference.

She laid down and put her arm across her forehead, shading her eyes from the sun. Sweat dripped off her legs, down her sides. When she was about to give up and go inside, he wheeled himself down the ramp. She turned to look at him. She had never looked at him so blatantly.

"How's it coming?" he asked.

"Okay," she said. "It's still disgusting, though." She sat up and put her shirt back on. She wondered what he'd do if she went and sat on his legs, if he could hold his knees together so she wouldn't fall. "He wants to take it to Cedars of Lebanon this weekend."

"I used to go there when I was a kid," he said.

"It's pretty crappy."

"I liked it. My whole family would go and we'd rent cabins."

She didn't say anything and turned her head away, so she was looking up at a tree. Then she looked back at him and said, "How old are you?"

"Twenty-eight," he said.

"You look older."

"Why do you say things like that?" he asked, and she told him she had to pee and then went inside and ran to the bathroom. It wasn't charming anymore, saying inappropriate things. Sometimes she'd tell people she had her period, as if it were a problem they might be able to solve.

She flushed and washed her hands and went back to the kitchen, listening for his wheelchair. He was quiet, as if he listening for her as well, and then his television came on too loudly and then the volume got quieter and quieter until she couldn't hear it any more.

"I wish I was drinking those," the man in the checkout line said. He had a banana in his hand. She had watched him carefully select it. She had a box of Heineken and a pack of cigarettes and it wasn't even noon. The man was in spandex, with his banana. He would eat it and bike up and down hills and he would not get leg cramps.

She went out to the car, her boyfriend waiting, and he drove them back to the campground.

He took off his shirt and walked the two steps to the other side of the trailer to rifle through the movies he'd brought. Then he took off his pants and looked at her. He liked to be naked but he didn't like to be naked when she was clothed. She didn't like to be naked. She took off her clothes and set them in a pile at the end of the bed and then stacked her pillow on top of his—dark green with safari animals. She breathed in the smell of piss and old bread, admired the back of him as he put in *Requiem for a Dream*.

"This is the most depressing movie ever," she said.

"It hasn't even started yet."

"I know but I've seen it and it's fucking awful."

"Why don't we watch something else then?" he said.

"No. I want to watch it," she said.

He pressed pause and opened the refrigerator that didn't work—the bar—and fixed himself a whiskey and Diet Coke. Then he took his one-hitter from the drawer and restarted the movie. The trailer filled with smoke. She was afraid someone would knock, though no one was going to knock. She was afraid the police would burst in and take them to jail and she'd have to call her father and he'd have to drive the four hours to come get her and he'd be disappointed.

On screen, Harry's mother was retrieving the television he'd pawned. Then she was eating a snow cone. She closed her eyes.

When the movie was over, they dressed and went

outside and sat under the tent he'd erected—their living room. Inside, there was a table and four chairs, as if they were waiting for their friends to arrive.

"I think I'll grill hot dogs," he said, moving things around. He set the grill up outside where she couldn't see him. He came back for the bag of charcoal and then disappeared again. The tent was a bad idea: she couldn't see the sky; the sides were strung together so no breeze got in. She imagined the other campers imagined them unfriendly, which made her feel unfriendly. She took a beer out of the cooler and looked at the bright white sides again, the narrow opening at one corner where she could see a swath of dirt and lake.

They ate on paper plates and drank cherry Kool-Aid and then they went back inside and got in bed. He rolled on top of her and she held onto him, thinking about the piece of cervix that the doctor had removed and whether that piece had been important. She had been pregnant once, but she'd miscarried during a football game and her husband hadn't wanted to take her to the emergency room, which was probably the worst thing he'd ever done to her. He had been a nice husband, really, a good husband, and she had left him, same as she'd left her ex-boyfriend, same as she would leave this one.

LEAK

There's a leak, I told him, it's right over my bed. He didn't believe me. I was a girl.

What's it look like? he said. He was reading cartoons. When he found a good one he'd pass the paper across the table, tell me to read it. He'd say, here, take a look at this, and I'd laugh, but I never thought they were funny. It was just the two of us and things had been difficult since I'd grown breasts, they came between us. He wouldn't let me sit on his lap anymore.

It looks like a bull's-eye, I said.

How many rings?

Several, it's pretty big and it's getting bigger.

I need to see it, he said, before I call the roofer and get an estimate.

Later, after lunch, I followed him upstairs to my bedroom. It's a leak, he said, his hands on his hips. He had salad dressing on his shirt, a wet spot where he'd tried to rub it off. I could see his chest hairs. It was like looking through a porthole. And there's one here, too, he said, pointing to a long thin one like a comet's tail, or the streak left behind by an airplane. I used to have a friend who put her hand over her heart every time she saw an airplane, but she switched to private school and I didn't see her anymore.

You didn't tell me about that one, he said. What about in the other room? Go look. I went. I knew what a leak looked like now.

I don't see anything, I called.

I'll call the roofer, he said, Bill has a guy.

What'll happen if we don't get it fixed?

The ceiling'll fall in, he said, and I reminded him that it was right over my bed, on the side I liked to sleep because I didn't like sleeping by the door, even with it locked because I was afraid of intruders.

He went back downstairs and watched men hunt turkeys on television. He had a little wooden box he practiced on. When his friend Bub called, he started cleaning his gun.

Aunt Pat lived next door. She barely did anything but sit on her couch all day long and wait for Uncle Bill to come home. I'd go over there and play with her dog because I didn't have a dog. I wanted a dog but my father said we weren't dog people.

I sat on the steps while Li'l Baby looked for a gumball. She only liked the ones with stems.

When she found a good one, we went back inside and she chased it around the living room while Aunt Pat clapped and said, Oh, Li'l Baby, get it! Get it, Li'l Baby! She told me she collected them on her walks and planted them all over the backyard like Easter eggs.

Why don't you invite a friend over? she said. She was always asking about my friends. What were their names? Did I want to invite one over? Was I popular? I got the feeling she didn't know why anyone would want to be my friend, and when I did invite someone over she acted like the girl was doing everybody a big favor.

I don't feel like it, I said.

You're too young to not be feeling like things, she said. I didn't know what to say to that. Li'l Baby flipped over on her back and stuck her legs in the air like an armadillo, dead on the side of the road.

She wants you to scratch her stomach, Aunt Pat said.

I scratched but my fingernails kept getting hung up on her nipples, so I rubbed. Her belly looked like the inside of a shell. You could press your ear to it and hear the ocean.

When do y'all leave? she said. We were going to Florida, like we did every year. We stayed in a house on the beach and ate seafood and went to the outlet malls, but my father wouldn't let me go in the water because once I got caught by a riptide and almost drowned and after that I got stung by a jellyfish and after that my mother died. Neither of us wanted to go, but we did it to show somebody something. Sometimes I felt like tossing myself down the stairs and letting my father clean up the mess. It was kind of like that.

Saturday, I said.

Where are y'all staying?

The same place we always stay.

A house?

It's yellow. There's an RV park nearby with a lot of old people.

That'll be nice. Maybe you'll make a new friend. Bill never takes me anywhere. He's so cheap, you wouldn't believe how cheap he is, she said. Everybody knew how cheap he was. Our ladder leaned against their house. He always needed to borrow a battery or shotgun shells or he couldn't find his saw.

Li'l Baby shredded her gumball, tore the stem off, so we went back outside and I sat there while she searched.

Bub brought his fat kid and donuts over on Saturday morning. He forgot we were leaving, or he didn't know. My father didn't tell him anything. They wore their camouflage and went out into the woods and got drunk, but they kept to themselves.

Sometimes they'd take me and the fat kid fishing but I never caught anything. You could be sitting right next to someone and the fish went to them every time. There was a trick to it. I figured they wanted me to figure it out for myself but I didn't want to think about fish, their gills and jelly eyes and the way they flopped about in protest while dying.

My father wanted a boy, like the fat kid, who was named Darrell. You could clonk him on the head and teach him to shoot guns and skin animals and as long as he didn't turn out to be faggot, things were easy.

Hey, Pocahontas, Bub said. Where's your dad?

In his study, I said, getting ready to go.

Go where?

The beach.

Oh.

Yeah.

Well that'll be fun.

The fat kid sat at the table and asked if we had any milk. My father came out of his study and clonked him on the head. Then he sat and opened the box of donuts. I got the milk out of the refrigerator and four glasses, passed them around. I'd recently learned to thaw meat and boil eggs. My father bought me a five ingredient cookbook and kept the refrigerator stocked with ground beef and chicken and I had to find something to do with it. Mostly I combined the beef with ketchup and onions and shaped it into a loaf, and the chicken I cut up and sprinkled with salt and pepper. He wanted me to fry things but I was afraid to fry.

The kid had his own personal bag of donut holes. He reached his hand in and popped them into his mouth one at a time.

I think this milk is bad, the fat kid said to me.

I'm not in charge of the milk.

My father picked up the gallon and said, June 13th. Still good.

Bub and the fat kid left and my father followed me upstairs and asked me questions: did I pack swimsuits, my toothbrush, t-shirts? Did I pack the beach towels? Did we have any sunscreen? What was the difference between sunscreen and sunblock and suntan lotion? I thought about the time my mother told me I better take a bath or I wasn't going to Florida because I didn't like to take baths and sometimes she had to threaten me and I took one and went to sleep but then she heard the water running in the middle of the night and found me in an inch of cold water and my father made her feel terrible about it the whole way down.

I'm pretty sure sunscreen and sunblock are

the same thing, I said. Suntan lotion is if you want to get a tan.

I don't want to get a tan, he said.

Okay.

You can get a tan if you want.

Okay.

We better get going here pretty soon.

I zipped up my suitcase and he carried it down the stairs and out the door to his open trunk. Then he put his suitcase in, a cooler full of Cokes.

Why don't you run over to Pat's and remind her to get the mail, he said.

I walked.

Aunt Pat, he said, was flighty. Aunt Pat was my mother's people. His people didn't come around. They were spread out all over, Arkansas and New Mexico and California, which made them easier to like. He had a sister who traveled the world on a boat with her sea captain husband. She sent us things through the mail: statues of Buddha, first edition books, turquoise bracelets. We gave them away to poor people, who had less use for them than we had.

I knocked and Uncle Bill opened the door. He handed me a plate of cookies Aunt Pat made and winked and I reminded him to get our mail and then I turned around and walked back to the car. I could feel him watching me. I looked back and he held up a hand but he didn't lift the corners of his mouth. He was a deacon at our church. I tried not to hold it against God. It wasn't God's fault that all the sick people in the world latched onto him.

She's going to get the mail? he said. He was crazy about the mail. He was also crazy about our property line. If someone parked in front of our house, he took down their license plate.

I told Uncle Bill.

Cookies, he said. What kind?

Looks like some kind of nut.

Hand me one, he said, backing out. I peeled the saran wrap off and gave him a broken one. Chocolate chip and pecan, he said, holding it up. I like Pat. That Pat's a good woman.

She's always acting like I don't have any friends.

You have friends.

Not that many.

You've got lots of friends. What about that little bowlegged girl?

She goes to the academy now.

Since when?

Since last year.

Oh, he said. Phyllis is your friend.

Phyllis lived around the corner. She was allergic to the sun. When I went over to her house we sat in the dark and played with dolls but mostly I watched the circles under her eyes grow. We were too old to play with dolls but Phyllis hadn't heard. She was home schooled.

If you've got one true friend that's all you really need, he said. I didn't know where he'd heard that load of crap but I'd heard it, too. It seemed like a bad idea, narrowing your options down to one.

Let's don't talk about it anymore, I said.

We stopped at Shoney's for lunch, the plastic Big Boy in the corner. The lady led us to a booth and my father sat down but then he got up to use the bathroom and the man at the next booth had no companion so we were facing each other. The man was wearing a red t-shirt with a tattoo creeping out of the neck of it. He smiled at me with straight white teeth and I looked away and then my father came back and sat down and I scooted over so he blocked the man.

I'm not really that hungry, I said.

You better eat. Who knows when we'll stop next.

I knew when we'd stop next, at five o'clock, for supper, but I said okay and ordered chicken fingers and my father ordered the catfish with greens and macaroni and cheese and cornbread. While we waited there was nothing to say but he felt the need to talk which meant he asked me questions he already knew the answers to. I didn't ask him anything. I could see straight through him. The red t-shirt man stood and opened his wallet, laid a bill on the table. He showed me his teeth for the last time and walked out to his Volkswagen Bug.

He looked so small and hunched over behind the wheel.

Our food came and I made myself eat because my father was disappointed when I didn't eat. He probably catalogued my needs in his head, checked them off one by one: food, water, shelter, love.

The people got trashier the farther south you went.

We pulled into a gas station in Navarre Beach and my father pumped gas while men toted cases of beer to their trucks. They smoked without hands and had wiry arms the color of old ground beef. Enormous women in tight clothes leaned against phone booths and parked cars, like they couldn't be bothered to hold themselves up anymore.

When we got to Panama City, I rolled down the window and breathed in the heavy air. We stopped off at the office for a key and then drove to the house.

I went to my room, put my suitcase on the bed and unzipped it. My clothes were jostled and hot. I checked the drawers to see if anybody'd left anything. Then I put my swimsuit on because the sun was still out. My swimsuit was last year's swimsuit. It was red with Coca-Cola written in cursive all over it. I tried not to ask for things because I was worried about money. I used to hear them arguing about it, where to put it, why there wasn't more of it.

I knew my father went to her grave to deposit flowers and I could see him kneeling there with his head bowed and I wanted to kneel beside him, but he wanted to protect me from death. He didn't know I could see it everywhere.

As soon as I got back, I went over to Phyllis's house. Her mother answered the door and called me Sugar, said Phyllis had been missing me something terrible. Then the phone rang and she left me standing in the open door. Something terrible got stuck in my head. I walked down the hall thinking *something terrible, something terrible.* Phyllis had been missing me something terrible. Phyllis's room had yellow walls and a dresser with a row of things I wasn't allowed to touch: bath salts and body lotion and soap shaped like ducks, but she didn't use them because once you used them they were worthless.

We sat on her floor with a stack of magazines. I stuck my legs straight out and pressed my fingers into them to call attention to my tan, but she flipped through the pages of her magazine without looking up.

The tops of my feet got burned, I said, though the burn wasn't a burn anymore. It was a pretty red-brown color, same as my arms and legs.

Look at the ears on this one, she said. The girl was straddling a horse in a string bikini, her hair slicked back so she was basically eyes and ears and the places where things should have been. It wasn't unattractive. Phyllis wanted to be a model but she was plump and white with just the tiniest hint of a nose. I could see her in a pot of water surrounded by carrots and potatoes.

She's not too bad, I said.

You're right, I'd trade.

I want to swing, I said.

When the sun goes down I can.

My dad likes to eat at five o'clock.

Maybe you can go home and feed your dad and then come back and spend the night.

I can't, I said, because I didn't feel like waking up in her house and wondering where I was, and I didn't feel like sitting at the breakfast table with her brothers while her mother asked if I wanted this, or that, or more of this, like she would give anything.

So come back tomorrow.

Maybe.

I'll call you, she said, and you'll come back.

Okay.

You better come back.

I will.

She walked over to her dresser and selected the smallest duck in the family of ducks. Here, she said. This is the baby. You can have it if you come back tomorrow.

It would have been easier to stay had she not wanted me to stay so badly. I walked down the hall and let myself out but then I heard her mother say something so I opened the door and her mother said to come back soon and I said I would. I took a left out of her driveway and walked down her street and then I took a right and was almost to my house when a boy passed on a bike. He flung his hair and circled back and flung his hair some more. I turned up my driveway. When I got to the door, I watched him push his bike up the street a ways before hopping back on.

My father was grilling hotdogs. I sat at the table and watched as he took them off the grill with his fingers, one at a time, furious. We had tongs but he looked for ways to suffer over and above all of the ways already in place.

He set the plate of hotdogs on the table. There were eight of them and two of us.

Would you fix us a couple of Cokes? he said.

I put ice in the glasses while he got the ketchup

and mustard out of the cabinet, the bag of buns. I checked the date smudged into the plastic to make sure they were still good.

After he finished his first one, he looked up at me and asked how Phyllis's was. I couldn't look at him. I looked out the window at the birds poking around the grass. A statue of a saint found lost things.

I don't like Phyllis anymore.

That's too bad. Phyllis likes you.

That doesn't mean I have to like her back.

No, it doesn't, he said. Then he told me to eat my hotdog and I told him I didn't like hotdogs and he said since when and I told him that hotdogs were like eggs. I'd never liked eggs but he kept giving them to me and I kept saying I didn't eat them and finally I broke down and started eating them.

And now you like them.

I don't like them. *I eat them.*

He repositioned his fork, his glass, centered the plate on his mat.

In the morning, Aunt Pat called. My father answered and she told him to send me over. I'd go back and forth, fetching things.

She waved me in and we stood in her kitchen. There was a cuckoo clock and a framed picture of connected stick figures: if mama ain't happy ain't nobody happy. There was a teapot and a grocery store cake and Li'l Baby laid out on the floor. She hobbled over to me like an old lady and I picked her up.

Li'l Baby is pooped, she said. We went for a walk. I made a chicken casserole. *Do you like chicken casserole?*

It's okay.

Everything with you is always okay.

I wanted her to just give me the damn casserole and let me go home but she was going to take an interest in me first.

Your father tells me you're having problems with your little friend, she said.

Which little friend?

The neighbor girl.

There's no problem.

If there's a problem, you can tell me about it.

Okay.

So?

She can't go outside because she has this thing with the sun. She's allergic.

And?

And I like to go outside.

I'm sure you two can work it out, she said. She gave me the casserole and told me to heat it for thirty minutes at three-fifty and serve it with a tossed salad and a loaf of French bread. Sometimes she unfolded the arms from my chest. Other times she just put things in them. After my mother died she took me to J.C. Penny's and bought me bras and I'd never really gotten over it, how she clutched my shoulders and told me I was spilling out all over the place.

I carried the casserole home and stuck it in the refrigerator. Then I found my father in his study with his shotgun on his lap. He'd been in the war, done something with radios, fixed them, or talked over them. It wasn't clear. Now he just broke down his gun and put it back together. Fish and deer were mounted on the walls and there was this smell like something rotting, but if I mentioned it he'd say a rodent must have crawled under the house and died. The fish had plaques underneath them like birth announcements: weight and date and who was responsible.

What'd Pat want? he said.

A casserole.

She wanted you to make her a casserole?

No, she gave me one.

What kind?

Chicken.

Chicken shit, he said. I'm sick of chicken.

The phone rang. I walked into his bedroom and sat on the side where my mother used to sleep. Sometimes I peeled back the covers and got in, the sheets so cold and clean, and stayed there for hours. It was Phyllis. She wanted to know where her duck was and I told her it was my duck now and she asked where *my* duck was and I told her I was looking at it that very minute, that I'd just snapped its head off and now that it was ruined I could use it.

My mom made haystacks for you, she said.

I found her on the floor with her laundry basket full of dolls. The dolls were mostly pieces of dolls because we popped the legs off at the hip, and sometimes the arms. She selected one with a haphazard haircut and made her hoist herself up into the pink van and sit there, wishing she had legs. She pushed the van around in circles. Vroom, vroom, she said. We called it the Love Bus because we made the legless dolls get in the back of it and eat each other out.

I kicked off my shoes. Her mother brought in a tin of haystacks and set them at my feet.

Phyllis popped them into her mouth whole. Then she opened her mouth and laughed. It sounded like it came from a place she had no control over. It made me nervous so I got up and went to the bathroom and sat on the toilet pinching the skin on my stomach. I fingered a mole to the left of my bellybutton and another one above it and wondered what a mole was and why I had so many of them.

When her mother came back the tin was empty except for a few loose straws, and since I was skinny, I told her I must have been really hungry because I'd eaten nearly all of them, and she smiled and said she'd make more. She was glad I liked them. I was just a little wisp of a thing. Bless my heart. Her mother went out and one of her brothers came in, the smaller one. He was wearing a silver jacket with tabs on the shoulders so you could pick him up and toss him.

Hey, he said to me. I smiled. Phyllis shrieked. Her brothers weren't allowed in her room without permission, which she never granted. He put his palm on the flat of the van and pushed it as hard as he could into the wall.

I was certain that whatever was wrong with her she'd brought upon herself.

I went home and waited for the lightning bugs to show up. I used to catch them and put them in a jar and watch them blink themselves out but now I just watched them. I saw the first couple of blinks and then I saw the boy come up the street. He got off his bike and dropped it on the grass and told me he had on a flame-retardant suit and he was going to light himself on fire. He struck a match and lit himself on fire, like he said he would, and he flamed up pretty good and then he flailed into the fence that divided our house from Aunt Pat's and a section of it came down and then he started rolling around while I sat there trying to mask my alarm and feeling like this was all my fault even though I'd done nothing wrong because this was clearly about me. I stood up and went inside but then I heard him scream so I looked out the window and saw that he'd managed to put himself out. He was in our grass on his stomach and I wanted it to be morning already so I could go over there and stand inside the outline of his body.

My father hadn't heard a thing. He was watching television. A man high up in the trees whispered into the camera. It was the first day of deer season, he said, so he wasn't going to get too excited.

We had a maid come three times a week. She had eleven children and her children had started having children. The circle of life, my father said, when we saw a bunch of lions kill an elephant on TV, when Deloris had another baby. In the mornings, the bus would let off and all the black women would walk to the houses they belonged to for the next six hours, and then you'd see them strolling the little white babies up and down the street but they didn't love the little white babies, you could tell, they cared for them but they didn't love them, not like I imagined I'd love a little black baby.

When Deloris came in, my father went out.

I sat at the table, looking out the window at a paunchy orange-bellied bird. Deloris moved her weight around the kitchen. She peeled off strips of bacon, cracked eggs.

She set the plate in front of me and I ate a piece of bacon but I didn't touch the eggs.

Eat them eggs, she told me.

I was sorry I'd ever eaten the first bite of an egg.

You is disappearin right before my eyes, she said, shaking her head.

I wanted to ride my bike but the tires were flat.

The boy who lit himself on fire was at the ditch, tying a rope to a blowup raft. He dropped the raft in the water and we stood there and watched it bob. He asked where I thought it would take him and I said to the river and then probably to the ocean.

That's cool, he said. I checked to see if his eyebrows were singed, leaned into his hair to see if it smelled like burned peanuts.

Where'd you get that raft? I said.

I have a pool.

That's nice.

It's not so great, he said. You can come over and swim in it if you want, see how boring it is.

When?

Now.

I have to go home. Deloris is probably wondering where I am.

Who's Deloris?

My maid. I stood there for a minute waiting to see what he'd do but he didn't do anything.

So go home then, he said.

Deloris's kids called all day long. They called during *The Young and the Restless* when something good happened. They called for no reason at all. My father said black people were often purposeless like this. He said you could go to any government office and just see them hanging around, using the bathroom and drinking from the water fountain and eating up all the free mints. There was this black boy at school named Terrance who sat behind me. He poked me with the eraser side of his pencil and I wanted to turn around but I just let him poke me and say, hey, hey, hey, hey, girl.

The phone rang. Deloris was upstairs, cleaning my tub. It didn't drain properly so all the dirty water stood at my ankles when I showered and nests of hair and grayish sludge gathered at the edges. It was Deborah. She was the only one whose name I could remember, but I pronounced it wrong. The accent was on the bor. I was always putting the accent on the Deb. Sometimes I asked

Deloris to tell me the names of her children and she'd reel them off. The first seven had names that started with D.

I called for Deloris, and waited for her to pick up, and then I went outside and walked through the hole the boy made and knocked on Aunt Pat's door. As soon as I saw her stiff hair and green pantsuit, I regretted it.

Oh, Li'l Baby, look who's here! She passed Li'l Baby to me.

Aunt Pat was my mother's older sister but my mother had never had much use for her. I didn't have much use for her by extension but I kept finding myself at her door, looking for what I'd lost.

Are you hungry? she said. Let's go to lunch.

Okay.

You pick.

Ruby Tuesdays?

The last time I went in there the service was terrible, you wouldn't believe how bad it was. I know this great little French place.

Okay.

Just let me grab my purse and we'll go, she said, and I stood there waiting for the second hand to get back around to the twelve: cuckoo, cuckoo, cuckoo. Li'l Baby jumped out of my arms and went to get her gumball. She tossed it and retrieved it and tossed it again. It wound up under the couch. She wouldn't go under things, or over them, so she just stood there barking.

Li'l Baby shit on the floor. That's what my father said when I mentioned her: that dog shits on the floor.

Aunt Pat's car was big and white with leather seats. There was nothing on the floorboards except an empty pill bottle rolling back and forth and I wanted to pick it up and put it in the glove box but I didn't. I moved as little as possible around her because she watched me so closely.

The little French place was full of old women. The girl led us to a table and I sat down while Aunt Pat visited with a group of women in hats. She pointed at me and I smiled and they gave me sorry looks so probably she was telling them I was her niece and my mother was dead and she was trying to do the best she could by me, but it wasn't easy because I was at that age. My mother used to sing at the retarded mass and I'd give them the same looks, like they were awfully sad and yet so brave! They had their own mass because they liked to get up on stage with the priest and take the microphone away from my mother and sing the same note over and over and that was all part of the show. It was their own special mass! So sad and yet so brave!

The women squawked from across the room, flopped their heads about on loose necks. Aunt Pat laughed and the women laughed and then she sat down across from me and unfolded her napkin.

So, she said. What're we having?

I don't know.

The quiche is good.

I don't like quiche.

What about chicken salad? You like chicken salad.

It's okay, I said.

Let's not be difficult, she said so brightly it made my teeth hurt. I wanted to be at home, on my mother's side of the bed where the sheets were cold and clean.

After lunch, we picked up Li'l Baby so we could drive her out to the country and a girl named Sue.

You're gonna get your hair did, Li'l Baby! Aunt Pat told her. She handed her to me; the dog rested her paws on my arm and I pinched at them. They were like tiny bear claws. I rolled down the window and stuck her head out. Her ears blew back and her heart beat so fast: bum, bum, bum, bum, bum, bum, bum. Aunt Pat yelled I was scaring her so I pulled her head in and rolled the window up.

On our way up the dirt drive, two country men stopped talking to watch us, a lawn mower between them. Sue came out of her trailer. She was small and young-looking but something about her was old. She was wearing an apron and smiling. Her hair stopped at her chin. She seems happy, I said. Aunt Pat said it was because she didn't have to pay taxes. We left Li'l Baby with her and drove around, stopping at a shop that sold candles and necklaces and things she called setabouts. She bought me a necklace I said I liked. It was beaded. I didn't really like it but I wanted to let her buy me something so I could see if she'd charge my father for every little thing.

After an hour we went back to pick her up. Li'l Baby looked especially bug-eyed and her lashes kept falling into her eyes. We told her how pretty she was, how special. She didn't seem to know what to make of herself. She was quiet and reserved, as if she had something valuable to protect, her reputation, or her virginity.

Deloris was eating her lunch when I came in. It was two o'clock and soon she'd pack her bag and lumber down the driveway and up the street while I waited for my father. Every day, she made a big show of eating one sandwich and drinking one can of Coke, but I walked in on her eating all day long. She ate spoonfuls of peanut butter and slices of cheese on white bread and sugar cookies. Sometimes I counted the cookies just so I'd know how many she'd eaten because she'd been with us since I was a baby and she didn't love me any more now than she did then.

My father came home and put on his shorts and walked outside to pick up the trashcans. Then he came back in and told me to turn the oven off. I could eat the baked chicken tomorrow or throw it away for all he cared. It was a relief. Everything in the five recipe cookbook tasted the same and if I used one of my mother's cookbooks, I'd have to make a list of things for him to get at the store and he had trouble getting things he didn't normally get. He'd come home missing the one item I couldn't do without, like the tarragon in the chicken with tarragon mayonnaise or the pineapple in the pineapple pork roast.

I sat outside with him while he drank his bourbon and Coke and watched the pigeons circle. They went round and round like they were on a track. The man who lived behind us kept them.

How come they always go back home? I said.

Because the man feeds them, he said, but I knew it was more than that. Then he asked if I'd make the potatoes so I went inside and ran a couple under the faucet, stabbed them with a knife and put them in the microwave. I went back out and waited for him to give me another assignment. He was a manager at a bank, and his job, he liked to tell me, was to make people want to do theirs.

He made me want to do a shitty job.

When the food was ready, we went inside and sat down.

I took my time dressing the meat with lettuce and pickles and mustard. I got up to get a slice of cheese from the refrigerator. Then I put it together before tearing it apart.

I was thinking you should go to the academy this year, he said.

That costs a lot of money.

You don't have to worry about money. Your mother left you money.

She did?

It'd be easier for me to take you in the mornings.

Okay.

You'd probably fit in better there anyway. The little bowlegged girl—.

Emily, I said, and I saw her standing on the soccer field with her hand over her heart as an airplane deposited its fluffy white strip across the sky.

The phone rang.

We looked at each other.

I told him not to answer it but he was incapable of letting a phone ring so he picked it up and said hello and hold on just a second, Phyllis, and handed it to me.

My dad's taking us skating, she said.

Twenty minutes later, I left my father in his chair with an ice cream cone. I hardly ever went out after dark. It was like falling out an open window.

Men swooshed past us skating backwards. They'd been planted there to show us how easy it was. Phyllis and I pumped away. She had on tight shorts, her legs thick and straight down to the ankle, and I hoped I wouldn't see anyone I knew because Phyllis was ugly and kids were liable to point this out. We skated together and then we skated apart to see who needed who more.

I was making the turn when she went down. She crawled over to the carpeted wall and lifted herself up. Her father put down his newspaper and smiled at her, brushed the hair from her face. I skated up beside her and asked if she was okay and she said she was and then I just stood there watching the two of them interact, how easy they were with each other. He wasn't afraid of her, of himself, what he might be capable of. He asked if we wanted something to eat and we said we did so he gave her a five dollar bill and we went and stood in line and ordered French fries and Cokes, ate them while everyone was gearing up for the Hokey Pokey.

My father was asleep in his chair when I got back.

Dad? Dad, dad. You wanna get in bed?

He opened his eyes and told me he was getting up, but he didn't budge. I turned off the lights and climbed the stairs, slept with my bra on.

In the morning, there was Deloris standing over a skillet of bacon. I fixed a bowl of Fruity Pebbles and sat down. She put the plate of bacon in front of me and I watched the strips soak through the paper towel.

You has got to eat, she said.

I am eating.

You has got to eat somethin other than cereals.

She sat down and rested her chin in her hand. Then she got up and opened the ironing board. It made a loud sound of protest. She turned on the small black-and-white TV and talked back to it. I went upstairs and got back in bed. There was the bull's eye and the long thin streak like a comet's tail. The roof hadn't been fixed yet. My father called the guy but he was busy until the first of August and my father hadn't bothered to call anyone else. I was hoping the ceiling would hold.

EVEN THE INTERSTATE IS PRETTY

My sister is inside watching a movie and bleeding. I don't bleed anymore. It's not something I thought I'd miss. My mother refers to the whole situation as my apparatus. When I'm quiet she asks if it's because of my apparatus, and sometimes, in the middle of a conversation, she'll put her hand on my arm and say, just because you don't have your apparatus doesn't mean you're not a woman.

I have pictures in my head of what my insides looked like before and what they look like now, but otherwise, I have difficulty with visualization. The lady who insists I call her by her first name tells me to visualize the beach or a rustic mountain scene and I try to connect the sand with the water, the mountain to the trees to the birds, but all I can do is repeat the names of them in my head. Sand, I tell myself, waves, but it's like describing the color of the sun to a blind man, or maybe it's not like that at all. Maybe he sees yellow every time he steps outside.

My sister opens the sliding glass door and sits down across from me in a chair shaped like an egg, lights a cigarette. Except for my bed, my furniture is modern and uncomfortable, impractical. My desk, for example, holds nothing, and my bookshelves hold books just fine until you go to read one. I pick up her pack, pluck out the one turned upside down for good luck.

That movie was fucked, she says, smiling. Why'd you make me watch it? I'm all depressed now. She stands and lets her hair fall over the balcony.

We change and take the elevator down, picking up a man with a small dog on the third floor.

He should paper train that bitch, she says, while we wait for a horse-drawn carriage to pass. I feel sorry for the horses, the dogs. They don't belong here with all the concrete, the homeless and parking garages.

We cross the street to the bar.

You again, the doorman says, not unfriendly, and I say, it's me, and then I walk straight back to the bathroom. I examine the contents of the trash can while I pee. There's a beer bottle among the tampon wrappers and ribbons of cellophane, my apparatus tangled up like a string of Christmas lights. And then my apparatus is intact inside my body, the head of a ram.

Already the stools next to her are occupied.

I sit beside the curly haired one and the bartender tosses me a napkin. I order a beer. My sister grabs my wrist and tells me to put it on her tab, so I say her name, Melissa, and he nods. The curly haired one laughs and I see his canine teeth, long and sharp and stark white. He closes his mouth and I want to pry it open again, but he angles away from me and then he lays a couple of bills on the bar and walks out. I move into his warm seat and watch Melissa take shots with what is clearly a musician. The city is full of them: sad white boys who imagine their sadness bankable. I encourage the ones I know to get on antidepressants, to take up running.

The crowd moves in and out while my sister and the boy kiss. He puts his hands on her face and I think about how it's a selling point when I first meet someone, when that someone is asking me about the things he's been instructed to ask me about. I lack the necessary equipment, I tell him, and the boy never asks questions, though I am prepared to give answers, have been waiting to give them. I open my purse and pull out one of my father's old handkerchiefs. I have other things of his—a watch, an expired driver's license—but I can't wave them above my head while hanging off a boat. I can't hold them the same way.

Melissa's been here over a week now. During the day she sleeps and watches *Meerkat Manor*, only goes out for chicken strips and cigarettes. At night, she walks across the street to the bar and I wake up to the sound of the couch becoming a bed. I listen to her whimper like something small and sick as a boy moves over her. Doors open, close. The boys' voices: I hear them clearly but I can't make out a word they say.

We're at MaggieMoo's and it's cold and there are no boys in here except for the big one waiting patiently for our order while we study the wall.

I'll have the Express Yourself, she tells him. He scoops the ice cream onto the slab of marble and folds in almonds and fudge. After he rings her up, he comes back to me and I can't say, S'more Fun than a Campfire. I want to say it but I can't. The campfire one, I tell him.

We sit at a table and look out the window.

Always some asshole in marketing coming up with shit to humiliate you, making you order an Ugly Naked Guy when all you want is a taco, I say.

What are you talking about?

S'more Fun than a Campfire? She shrugs. I shrug. I talked to mom earlier. She wants to know when you're coming home.

There's nothing for me there, she says.

She needs you.

Why's it have to be me?

Because you're the baby, I say. Because I have a life, I mean, and you don't. But then there's the question of what a life entails. I have a job that doesn't pay very well and friends I never see. I still sleep in my ex-boyfriend's t-shirt. There are magnets on my refrigerator and a clutter of pizza coupons in my drawer. Is this a life?

I was thinking I'd move here, she says. I like it here. Everything's so green and hilly. Even the interstate is pretty.

With me?

I guess not.

My place is too small.

I think my boobs are getting bigger. Are they getting bigger? They feel *huge*. She looks down at one and then the other of them and I look over at the big boy. He's got his chin in his hands, mooning over my sister, her heavy eye makeup and tight jeans, the hair piled on top of her head with bobby pins. Our mother wanted sorority girls, debutantes. She wanted to plan weddings and baby showers, but she refuses to be disappointed in herself so she acts like we were her design: a couple of pale-skinned girls with holes in their noses; one of them incapable of having a baby and the other capable only of mistakes.

On the way home, we stop to pick up beer and Diet Coke, and then we sit in front of the television watching *Animal Precinct*. A man and a woman in a van go around collecting neglected dogs. They spend weeks fixing them up and then end up putting most of them down because they have poor temperaments—they're food aggressive; they won't let you hug them; they stay riled up long after you've quit riling them. They may as well have left them chained up and starving.

An emaciated dog limps around in the snow, one of his back legs curled up. There's a blizzard coming. The owner of the dog isn't home and when he finally gets there he tells the animal cops the dog isn't his, that he is keeping the dog for a friend, and the two animal cops, the man and the woman, their hands are always tied. They stand side by side and look into the camera and tell us they do their best, they save the ones they can, but we don't believe them.

When it's over, I turn off the television but we don't move. After a while, she gets up and goes to the bathroom. I follow her, wash my face while she digs around in her makeup bag.

I pick up the shadows and blushes one at a time and read the names of them: Night Star, Ashes to Ashes, Orgasm, Sin.

I let her line my eyes with a gray crayon, smudge the edges with her fingertips. I stare at the wall, at a black-and-white picture of two girls on a beach. There are some people I can only look at from a distance, the people I love. She applies mascara to my bottom and top lashes, saying, look up, look down, open your eyes wide, blink.

You should try and look easy sometimes, just for fun, she says, kicking my dirty tennis shoe with her bare foot. In order to make boys love you, you have to trick them first.

I know how to make boys love me, I say, and she shakes her head all sad-like.

Karaoke night. After three shots and a beer, she's sitting on the bar with her legs swinging. I still can't see a goddamn thing, she tells me, moving her head around, though there is nothing to see but a man in a blue jean vest singing *Born to be Wild*. The bartender asks her to get down but she ignores him. Then the doorman comes over. He is thin and dark-haired with circles under his eyes like old bruises. I don't know his name but I feel like something is built every time our eyes meet. I want a whole city underneath us, before.

What's wrong with her? he says.

She's drunk.

I can see that.

Our dad died.

Oh. I'm sorry.

It's okay, I say, and I'm reminded of all the times I've walked in on women in public rest-rooms, how I say I'm sorry and they say it's okay and I feel like it's their own damn fault because they didn't lock the door but I'm the one who's supposed to feel badly about it.

She's been here every night this week, he says. I nod and a sidewalk is poured. Dogs traipse through the cement before it can dry. Melissa kicks off one of her heels and it goes flying. I wait for him to tell me I should get her some help but he just walks over and picks it up, holds her arm as he slips it back on her foot.

He points to himself and says, Tony.

Melissa, I say, Audrey. I'm relieved when no one says it's nice to meet you. I'm tired of say-ing it's nice to meet you, tired of greeting people over and over again like this man I used to work with who thought he had to say hello every time we passed so we were helloing all day long. Hello, hello, hello, hello, hello.

Tony lights our cigarettes. Then he goes back out to his stool where he sits and recruits passers-by. Melissa hops off the bar. She asks for another drink but the bartender won't serve her, so we pay our tab and walk out the open door.

Once I've passed him I turn around and hold up my hand.

Y'all be good, he says.

An Italian boy named Tony, she says to him, how original. I bet you've got a brother named Joe.

We call him Joey.

Come over later, she says, bring me a box of Camel Lights. I'm out.

He looks at me.

We're probably going to bed soon, I say, and he tells us to take it easy, crosses and uncrosses his arms.

You hurt his feelings, she says. He wanted to do you. Poor guy, he's all tore up now. You should just let him do you.

We take the stairs up.

Inside, I open a couple of beers and we go out to the balcony and drink while down below, Tony looks right and left. I watch him knowing he knows we're up here, knowing he won't look up, and I think about another Tony, a shorter fatter one, and how, every morning, this Tony would sit on the toilet at the same time saying you could train your bowels to shit on command but then he'd stay in there forever reading an almanac, would emerge with something for me to consider. What's the difference between partly sunny and partly cloudy? he'd ask, or he'd tell me what happened on that day in 1863. This other Tony worked maintenance at a hospital and we'd go up to the roof and hang our heads over the edge and talk about how great it was to be up so high, and I liked him because he wore a tool belt and my father had never fixed anything, because pretty early on he'd admitted to wanting to impregnate me and every other boy I'd ever been with took me out for margaritas when my period came, fed me quesadillas and guacamole and expected me not to get fat.

A car stops in the middle of the street. The music goes boom, boom, boom. The boy in the passenger seat gets out and goes around to the trunk, stands there waiting for it to open. The driver honks. The boy gets back in. The driver peels out.

Hey, she calls down to him. He looks up, hey yourself. We're looking down at Tony, who's looking up at us and then he's in my apartment, standing there with a box of Camel Lights for my sister, a bottle of wine for me. It was in my car, he says, shrugging. We feed him shots of vodka and amaretto, to catch up, and move him around the apartment like something exquisite we have no place for.

FAST TRAINS

He had an air gun, a beer box set up to shoot. We were in a hotel room in Pigeon Forge. He was proud because our room was right by the entrance, the TV had HBO, and from seven to ten every morning there was a continental breakfast. He had the alarm on his phone set for twenty minutes till so we wouldn't miss it.

I was flipping through a magazine while he messed with his gun, which kept getting jammed. I had a stack of magazines with the covers ripped off: *Maxim*, *Bust*, *Shambala Sun*. I got them free at work, once the new ones came in.

"Do you think you can hit the box?" he said.

I can hit the box, I thought. He handed me the gun and I aimed and pulled the trigger. I hit something and the ball ricocheted.

"Did you hit it?"

"I don't know."

"I think you hit it," he said.

"This thing is dangerous. You could put an eye out."

I set his gun on the bed and handed him my glass.

We were drinking his good whiskey because we were on vacation. He was cheap and I felt bad drinking his good whiskey because our relationship was unstable and the things that were his were his and the things that were mine were mine but I didn't have anything he wanted. He said he only wanted my love but he'd say this after I'd failed, once again, to be what he wanted.

"Lots of ice," I said. "And some water. Not too much Coke."

He delivered my drink and then he went out to the balcony to get high.

When he came back, I held out my arms and he walked over and put his tongue in my mouth. I liked the taste of marijuana on him, like barbeque chicken left out overnight. I stuck my finger in the hole in his pajama pants, felt the skin and hair. His shirt had Homer Simpson walking a pig upside down on an invisible roof. SPIDERPIG, it said.

He sat on his side of the bed and turned the television to the History Channel. A group of large women were looking for Big Foot. They wore oversized sweatshirts and hats; they were the kind of women who had no use for men. I had never had any contact with this kind. He went to the bathroom, left the door open so I could watch his back in the mirror while he peed. He cleared his throat, spit into the toilet. His hair was thick and curly. I liked separating the curls into smaller curls. I liked separating the smaller curls into smaller and smaller curls until his hair was enormous and he had to wear a baseball cap to flatten it back down.

"Do you have any lotion?" he called.

"Hold on," I said. I turned my magazine upside down and then I went in there and opened the tiny hotel bottle of lotion. I dropped it and it spilled. I wiped it up with a tissue. I put a dollop on my finger and rubbed. It was just one of his balls that got dry. I knew which one. It made me think we should stay together forever.

He pulled up his pants and went down the hall to get ice, came back saying the hot tub was hot. Last night, it hadn't been hot. We'd sat in it while a family of five watched.

Back in bed, he shot into the corners of the room. He shot at the beer box on one side and a donut and bag of chips on the other. They were things he couldn't eat because he was on Atkins.

"I should throw that donut away," he said.

"So throw it away."

"I want to eat it."

"So eat it then."

"I shouldn't eat it."

"So throw it away."

"I don't know," he said. "I want it. It's a paradox."

"A real quandary," I said. I wasn't sure if it was a paradox. I couldn't remember what a paradox was. At work I had to write everything down, carry around scraps of paper.

Earlier, we'd driven into Gatlinburg. He bought me a slice of peanut butter fudge and bought himself a gold brick of diabetic fudge and we ate them while walking slowly and looking blankly at the people who were looking at us. We ignored the high-pitched calls of girls in boxes who wanted us to buy timeshares. One of the box-girls asked if we were newlyweds and I called over my shoulder that we were and smiled and swung my hair so she could see how happy I was.

I had a little bit of fudge left. It was in a white bag, behind the ice bucket. I ate it fast before I could think better of it.

"I'm going to have to eat that donut now," he said, as if it were my fault.

He took a big bite and then he shoved it deep into the trashcan so it couldn't be salvaged, like I did with my cigarettes sometimes before I went out and bought another pack.

"We should get ready," he said. "We're going to be late."

We were supposed to go to a show his sister had gotten us tickets for. I'd seen the brochure:

three middle-aged men in stage outfits and an audience full of old people. His sister was in the travel business. She had access. The room, for example, he'd gotten free. I saw the coupon that awarded it to us like we'd won something. He hadn't meant for me to see it.

"I don't want to go," I said.

"We have to. She's going to call me tomorrow and ask about it."

"I don't want to, though."

"I can't lie and say we went."

"You don't have to lie."

"I'll have to come up with a good reason," he said.

"Nobody ever believes your reasons," I said. He looked offended so I added, "Not yours in particular, just anybody's," and I reached across the bed and put a hand on his shoulder. The bed was king-sized. I moved my stack of magazines to the floor and scooted next to him. It was dark out, and cold, and I didn't feel like putting on my jeans, which would be too tight because they'd just been washed.

"I don't really feel like going, either," he said.

"Tell her I was too drunk or feeling mentally unstable. Those are the only things people believe, anyway."

"I'm not telling my sister that."

His gun jammed again and he cussed it. It

was settled, we weren't going. I fixed myself another drink and got back in bed and rested my head on his chest between sips.

I asked if we'd get married and he said we would. I asked if I could have his baby and he said I could. After that all I could think to ask was when.

"Soon," he said.

"How soon is soon?"

"I don't know how soon soon is. When do you want it to be?"

"July."

"Okay," he said, and I was relieved, knowing his willingness was all that I required of him.

We kissed for a while but we couldn't have sex because I was on my period and blood on his penis disturbed him.

"Suck my dick," he said.

I pawed at his jeans but I couldn't make myself do anything but yank at them so he made himself available. He pressed my head down and I gagged. He had watched a lot of porn. Once we watched it together but he said I ruined it because I kept talking about the women, wondering what their lives were like and how much they were getting paid, commenting on whether they were enjoying themselves. When my jaw began to ache, I varied my movements and pace but I knew I was only prolonging things.

Finally he was finished. I watched his body convulse, and then, because I was feeling mean, called attention to a raw spot on his ball.

"Don't look at it," he said. "It's ugly."

I was the only person who really knew him, he'd told me, but after six months he still felt brand new. I knew enough facts that I could present a decent-length paper, a timeline of major events, but when he put his hands around my neck, I couldn't say for sure he wouldn't kill me. No one knew the real me, either—all of my relationships had been the kind where they think they're seeing the worst of you but it's only a distraction. I had successfully hidden myself from everyone I'd ever known.

We went to the bathroom and cleaned up, got back in bed and watched a program about UFOs that come out of the water, USOs, they called them. They convinced me easily: Big Foot, women who didn't need men, USOs.

"Hey," I said.

"Hey," he said.

"Let's get in the hot tub."

He put on a pair of shorts because he'd forgotten his swimsuit, which reminded me of the boyfriend before him who was so poor he didn't even own a swimsuit, who lived off me and ate my food and drank my beer and I'd kept him around for months because he'd been imported from

Canada and neither of us had the money to send him back there. It was a bad time. I'd gotten rid of everything I had and replaced it with less.

The pool area was empty, the concrete wet where people had recently been. The hot tub wasn't hot but it was hotter than it had been last night. I sat in his lap and floated to the top when he wasn't holding me down. I stuck a leg out and turned it this way and that so he could admire me.

"You're beautiful," he said.

"I'm okay."

"You're beautiful to me."

I wanted to tell him I was beautiful to a lot of people, half the boys at work were in love with me. "I'm better-looking than your exes," I said. I'd met one of them at a party the weekend before. Thick with not-quite-blonde hair, she'd watched the rest of us play poker.

"Angela used to have a body on her," he said.

"It's not just her body. It's her face."

"What's wrong with her face?"

"Her skin is the color of under-eye circles."

He said I was being overly critical. It was an accusation we passed back and forth. I'd have to wait for him to say something terrible about someone so I could give it back to him.

He got out and dove into the pool, emerged below the no diving sign. "It's fucking freezing," he said. He got back in the hot tub, saying the hot tub was hot now. If I was cold I should get in the pool and then come back and it'd be hot.

"I'm tired," I said.

A family came in. Loud and heavy-footed, they probably still threw trash out their car windows. My boyfriend said hey and they said hey back. I looked the other way. I didn't like to talk to people, had nothing to say to them. They arranged their chairs in a circle and we sat there a while longer so it wouldn't look like they'd run us off and then we got out and dried off and went back to our room.

The next day, we woke to his alarm. I didn't want to get out of bed. He prodded me.

"No," I said, "uh uh."

He brushed his teeth and slipped on his house shoes.

"Would you get me a bagel?" I said.

"I need both sets of hands," he said, holding his set up. He reminded me how well it worked yesterday, when he got the plates and I got the drinks. I pretended to go back to sleep and he left. I lay there and thought about toasting his wheat bread and pouring Splenda in his coffee, how happy it would make him, and how the thought of his happiness didn't particularly please me. He was gone a long time.

He kicked the door and I went and let him

in. He had a tray with two plates and two coffees on it.

After we ate, he got high and then we went to the knife store. It was enormous. I followed him around offering comments, asking questions.

There were some handmade purses and jewelry along one wall. I stopped and he kept walking, touching everything he passed. The purses were Indian-patterned with snap closures. I liked a zipper closure but I tried to talk myself into one because I wanted to buy something. I liked to watch the money in my account dwindle. So far, there had always been enough and I anxiously awaited the day when there wouldn't.

I asked the lady to show me different worthless things from her case and decided on a pair of tiny sterling silver lizard earrings. I liked the elephants better but my mother had warned me to avoid all animals associated with bigness: hippos and pigs and elephants, in particular. They were only four dollars. After that I looked at Rebel flag t-shirts and thought terrible things about the people who vacationed in Pigeon Forge and then I found my boyfriend and he walked me around the store showing me the things he wanted: a cane with an eight ball on top that unscrewed to reveal a poker; a set of three swords in small, medium, and large; a pocket knife that had a picture of a man's face and the name of a bourbon he liked.

He said he had to think about them, though, he wasn't ready to make a purchase, so I made him drive me to the Gap outlet where I tried on a pair of khaki pants I could wear to work. He offered to buy them but I declined. In his head, if not on paper, there was a column with my name on it and how much I had cost him to date. There was the question of my worth—a complex equation involving my weight and breast size and hair length along with my willingness to engage in oral sex and my domestic abilities, of which I had none. I was okay on the others but I didn't know how long my body would consent to staying the size I had forced it into. It was the x in the equation.

We ate at a pancake house and then he stopped at BP, parked and ran inside to take a hit off his hitter, came back reeking. I didn't like him to smoke in the car. I didn't like him to smoke around me period but what I would and wouldn't allow changed and expanded.

"You probably stunk the whole place up," I said.

"I'm sure nobody noticed," he said, circling the station. His theory was that everyone was too busy worrying about themselves to notice anyone else, which was easy for him to believe because he had no sense of smell. Cocaine had taken it. Sometimes I forgot what it was he'd lost, imagined him blind or deaf or unable to feel my skin.

After that there was nothing to do so we drove back into Gatlinburg, through the town full of motels and fudge shops and box-girls, and stopped at a trailhead. We were all bundled up. We stood before a plaque that said a farmer used to live there and the trail was easy. I followed him in, watching my feet. I saw myself slipping and going down, my mouth bloody and the teeth I loved so much loose, as if in a dream. It'd be dark in an hour. Every time I found myself in the woods it was the case.

The trail wasn't easy. We were okay, we told each other, but we felt bad for the old women and children who had been misled. I picked up an icicle and slammed it into a rock. It shattered like glass. He stopped and looked at me and I smiled.

We came upon the man's house, a structure too big for the two rooms it housed. We went inside one room and walked the perimeter. There was a fireplace on one side and a window on the other. A few people had left their marks. The wind whistled through the logs. We walked over to the other room and it was the same thing backwards. He took my gloved hand in his and we went out to the porch, stood there looking at the side of a mountain. "What'd this guy farm?" he asked me. *A rhetorical question*, I thought. We kept moving, round and round until we were back at the car. Then we drove back down the mountain and through Gatlinburg and into Pigeon Forge, to our hotel dressed up like an antebellum home.

Our room had been tidied while we were away: a fresh set of towels and the toilet paper folded into an arrow.

I went down the hall to get ice. He liked a lot of ice, couldn't even drink cold things without it. When I got back, he was shirtless and in bed, watching the weather blow across the country.

"Looks like we might get snowed in," he said.

"I have to go to work on Tuesday."

"Well I do too," he said, like he had been accused.

I fixed him a drink, got a beer from the little refrigerator for myself. He said he was hungry so I made us a couple of sandwiches from the stuff he'd packed: chicken, bacon, double fiber wheat bread, cheese, mayonnaise. He liked meats, especially, and creamy things, the way they felt on his tongue. This works, he told me. He'd make the food and I'd put it together. Then he took it back because it wasn't a fair trade. I'd be getting off too easy.

I read an article about loneliness in a Jesus magazine while I ate. None of my coworkers believed in Jesus. We made fun of the earnest and plain-looking women who congregated in the religious section, one of them offering advice while the other protested mildly, their quilted Bible covers in paisley prints. Sometimes I got the urge to join them. It wasn't because there was something missing. The something missing was the plight of humanity—any idiot knew that—it couldn't be filled with food or alcohol or drawing blood from skin. I just missed having friends.

When he was finished, he moved to the couch and extracted his guitar from its case. He tuned it and made up a song about drinking, the same few chords over and over, his voice straining. All his songs were about fast trains, people running themselves out. Next door, I heard a baby cry and a woman's angry voice and I recalled the footsteps of the couple who lived in the apartment above me. I'd grown attached to the flushing of their toilet and the fights they had, the way the woman was always proclaiming herself done.

I got another beer and put on my jacket to go outside. He slipped on his house shoes.

He sat in one plastic chair and I sat in the other and he took hits off his hitter while I smoked my cigarette. Then we went back in and laid down, my head in his armpit, the TV off, like we were waiting for something. His phone rang. It was his sister, wanting to know how we'd liked the show. I could hear her saying we should have gone, we missed out on the best show in town, she didn't know why she went to the trouble. I'd met her at Christmas. She had given me a nightgown that was too big, and I hadn't written her a thank you note yet, was waiting to find out if it had been required.

He hung up and said, "See?"

"See what?" I said.

I got in the shower. He got in with me and we took turns standing under the water while the other complained that they were cold and chicken-skinned. When we were clean, we stood sideways so we could share the hot water for a minute. Then we got back in bed, and he sat in front of me while I brushed his hair. There was a comedian on TV. The audience laughed at every little thing because the man was already famous. I wanted to laugh, repeated the funnier things out loud to try and convince myself.

"Your hair's long enough for a ponytail now," I said.

"The front's still too short," he said, holding up a piece of it. I didn't know how it had become layered. He only cut it once every five years, and that was to shave it all off. He kept the hair in a box in his closet, tucked away like a child's lost teeth or a dead man's handkerchiefs. I'd met him one year into the cycle, while he still looked normal. It was a long-term project, he said, and one day he would donate all the hair to Locks of Love and before they gave it to the cancer children they would display it at a museum as a timeline of one man's life. A timeline of all of the chemicals you've ingested, I'd said, when he told me, and then I got mad because he wasn't going to change. I had been able to change the other men I'd been with, or at least they let me believe I could.

I opened another beer. There were only four left and the bottle of whiskey was almost done. I went and stood at the window. My car had a thick layer of ice on the back windshield.

"I'm getting drunk," I said.

"You're on vacation," he said. He stood and put on his jacket.

"You've been high this whole time."

"I just take a couple of hits." He went out and came back a minute later saying he'd only brought the equivalent of two joints and he still had some left. I was bent over the sink, washing what was left of the makeup off my face, when he shot me.

"Ow," I said. "That hurt."

"I shot myself in the foot twice and didn't feel a thing," he said. To demonstrate, he shot himself in the leg. There was a small pause while he made his assessment, and then he said, "That stings pretty good." He concluded that the feet didn't hurt but the leg and the ass hurt because they weren't as bony. "I'm sorry," he said. "Do you forgive me?"

"Yes," I said, and he went and sat on the couch like he believed me. He played his song—whiskey in the morning and beer in the afternoon, fast train clipping along—while I cried without making a sound. I wanted him to hear me but I was quiet, so quiet he wasn't going to find me out.

PEARL

At the breakfast table my mother said the world was my oyster.

"While I'm still young and pretty," I said.

My father didn't think the world was my oyster. I could tell by his silence he thought I should ask my husband to come back.

I'd had to move back home. Once there, things took up where they left off. My parents wanted to know where I was going. They felt obligated to tell me where they were going. I didn't care where they were going, though I liked to know when they were gone.

My friend's father called and said they were looking for a receptionist at his law firm so I went and answered the telephones. I liked to think it was temporary. I wore short skirts and high heels and pantyhose. Pantyhose were expensive. They snagged and ripped but I couldn't bring myself to throw them out. They used to come in eggs but now it was envelopes.

At work, I put my nails in my mouth and bit

down. They were healthy and strong and the tips white like a French manicure.

One of the partners would come and sit on my desk, take my hands out of my mouth. He had the start of a comb over, and the whites of his eyes were laced with bright red like they'd been shattered. His wife was an alcoholic, he told me, his daughter depressed, manic, depressed. They took turns unraveling and getting well and all of his money was tied up in property and retirement and he was cash poor and his father was dead and his mother was dead and his brother was dead. I let him talk and talk, didn't let on that he could bend me over right there, that I didn't need to hear his sob story. He had no idea how small my world had become.

His name was Robert but everyone called him Bob. I called him Robert. I had a problem calling anyone Bob. I didn't like palindromes. It was too abrupt. "Bob, cob, lob, rob, sob," I said, by way of explanation.

My birthday was coming up. It was as good excuse as any.

I met him in a restaurant inside a giant mirrored ball on the twenty-fifth floor. The ball was on top of a hotel on top of a casino. I was worried. My pants were white, my period set to start. I'd left my parents in front of the television. Every penny I spent was mine.

After dinner, we were going to gamble, he said, and I'd be his lucky charm. This also worried me. Gambling required a delicate balance of desperation and delusion, and I wasn't feeling much like deluding myself.

"I don't know how lucky I feel," I said.

"You're not the one who's got to feel it," he said, leaning forward.

I shifted in my chair, refolded the napkin on my lap. In liquor stores, I still got that sinking feeling left over from high school: hair too flat and nose all wrong, the license expired. He ordered a bottle of champagne.

The waitress left us alone for a long while, a father and his daughter out for a graduation celebration: the presentation of a fat check, or the keys to a BMW. When she returned, Robert ordered a filet mignon and a baked potato. I surprised myself by asking for the same. I didn't eat steak. I ate chicken, tofu. I drank soymilk.

He asked me about books, what kinds of books I liked. He'd seen me reading in the break room at lunch. I could see it had just occurred to him that he might ask me a question.

"I like books about fucked-up people," I said. "The kind you have to tear the cover off because there's a girl on the toilet staring at her shadow."

Our salads came. I ate but I wasn't hungry.

I hadn't been hungry since my husband left. I thought about my mother's sister, the one named after a dessert, and how she was still praying for my husband to impregnate me. She prayed to St. Jude, she told me, the patron saint of lost and hopeless causes, and I didn't mind being lost but hopeless bothered me. Hopeless was going too far. Someone was going to have to tell her.

We ate in silence, then rode the elevator down and made our way, weaving in and out, to the tables. Blackjack was his game. I kept a hand on him because it was crowded and I was in the way, so people could see that I belonged. A part of me wanted him to win and a part of me wanted him to lose and a part of me wondered what my husband had eaten and whether he'd taken a shit and how many cigarettes he'd smoked.

We went to the bar in the middle of the casino, water coming down the walls.

"We should stay the night," he said. He still had chips in his pocket. I could hear him rattling them around.

"I'd have to call my mother."

"You're a big girl now."

"I keep forgetting," I said.

"So I'll get a room and we'll stay. Two beds? One? Your call. If you're not comfortable—"

"I don't feel like calling," I said.

His shoulders sank. I went to take his hand

but he stood and brushed the front of his pants like there were crumbs all over him. "Stay right there."

"I'm not going anywhere."

"Don't move." And then he was gone but he was coming back. I thought maybe I'd move down a seat. The bartenders were young and female, fake breasts and blonde hair. One pretty, one plain. But maybe the plain one only needed more makeup, or maybe she would have been pretty on her own, without the comparison. It was hard to say. I felt sorry for her. It was her face.

Robert came back with two keys. He handed me one, took out his wallet and opened it. Worn brown leather, soft.

"Here," he said. "Go play. Have fun."

I put the bill in the machine, which gave me smaller bills, and then I went and sat at a different bar and slipped a twenty into a video poker machine. The bartender looked military. He fixed my drink, put his elbow on the bar. He watched me but he didn't comment. I was sure they weren't supposed to comment.

"You're making me nervous," I said.

"Is this all it takes?"

"Less."

I looked up and he started talking. He was in the Guard. I didn't know anything about the Guard except that once I asked my father about

Vietnam and he said the people who joined it were the lowest of the low. He'd be gone soon, he told me. He had no one to leave and no one to come back to and he used to be sort of fat with a ponytail but now he didn't have any fat on him and he was practically bald and it was strange living in a body he didn't recognize.

"That's interesting," I said.

"I know, I know," he said. "You don't want to hear my story." He ran a hand over his head. I imagined he could still feel the hair between his fingers.

"Tonight I'd like to talk to someone who doesn't have a story. Someone who loves their mama and their dog."

"I love my dog," he said.

"What kind?"

"Yellow lab."

"That figures," I said. "Hey. What should I do here?"

"Just the Ace. Dog's sweet, fixed. Loves to walk. You can keep him for me while I'm gone."

"I can't keep your dog," I said. "What the hell's wrong with you?"

He went to the other side of the bar to serve an older couple and then he came back and told me his name was David.

"Jillian," I said.

"I was kidding about you keeping my dog.

My ex-girlfriend's going to keep her. She's a great person."

I nodded and he said that actually she was a total bitch but she liked animals. I smiled. He showed me his back and I stopped playing and waited for him to look at me and then he did and I didn't look away like I usually do because there wasn't any time for it.

I pointed at my drink and he fixed me another.

"Are you taking a break anytime soon?" I asked, and then I was following him down a brightly lit hallway and I could see my drink sitting there, sweating, wondering when I'd be back. The walls were white and blank and the hallway so long I couldn't see the end of it and all I could think to say was that the tunnel was like death but I didn't say that because already I could hear it hanging in the air above us and then he stopped and took a key from his pocket.

Boxes everywhere. I pulled his shirt out of his pants and ran my hand over his stomach, which was flat and brown like the boxes, and he lifted his arms and leaned forward so I could pull it off and then he was kissing my neck, my mouth, my cheeks, my eyelids, which was sad and unexpected and made me think he thought he wasn't coming back. He wanted me to keep his dog and I thought maybe I should instead of letting his ex-girlfriend have him because already I had taken a strong dislike to this ex-girlfriend.

He unbuttoned my pants and spun me around and I waited for him to put a condom on while I thought about my number, skyrocketing, two men in one day. I wouldn't have enough hands to count. I wanted a cigarette. He felt between my legs and said how wet I was and opened me up and stuck himself inside me and this went on for some time, I don't remember how long it went on but I was there among the boxes and the white light and he was going to Iraq where he would need someone to write a letter to and I wanted to be the recipient of his letters and it made me think of Harry Potter and all those letters pouring in, you couldn't stop them, no matter what you did you couldn't stop them. I wanted his letters and I wanted to walk his dog every morning and I'd lose fifteen pounds while he was away and then he'd come home and think I was the most beautiful thing he'd ever seen, or else he wouldn't come home and I'd still be thin and I'd still have his dog. Either way.

"My boyfriend's probably looking for me," I said, because it seemed like he was having a hard time so I thought maybe I'd help him out even though I was close, maybe just another minute, but I felt like fucking everything up because it was so easy to fuck up and he wouldn't be able to do a damn thing about it and I didn't really want his dog or his letters. I didn't really want his love.

I took the bed by the window and turned on the television. I wasn't too drunk. I set my phone on the table and waited for it to ring.

It was my mother. I told her I was spending the night out. She wanted to know where and I said it was none of her concern, which made it her concern, so I told her I'd had too much to drink and was staying at Polly's because I wasn't divorced yet and my mother didn't understand technicalities. My husband wasn't coming back, and I wasn't going to ask him to come back even if it made me complicit in his leaving.

Robert came in late, stumbling, his shirt untucked. He stripped down to his underwear, and fell into the other bed facing me. He folded his hands under his cheek like a child and I could see his shattered eyes and his nose, crooked and bulb-tipped, and I knew he was just like the rest of them.

"I'm not going to touch you," he said.

"How come?"

"You remind me of someone."

"Your daughter?"

"I thought I'd do better by her," he said.

The air conditioner clicked on. I wondered

if my mother believed I was staying at Polly's. I knew she didn't, but then tomorrow, when I told her where I'd really been, she'd act genuinely surprised.

I'd been trying out the truth lately and people didn't like it. I wasn't sure how I felt about it yet. It made messes of things that didn't require a mess.

"I'm sure you did what you could," I said.

"As soon as she was born, I was done with her."

"You were probably just afraid."

"That wasn't it," he said.

"We're all afraid, but see, men, they get violent when they're afraid."

"I'm not a violent person."

"That's why you have to go and fuck yourself up," I said.

He didn't say anything and then he said maybe I was right and I wanted to say something to make him feel better but I couldn't think of anything. I listened to him breathe. I pictured myself waking up in a few hours and sitting on his bed: my finger beneath his nose, ear to his chest, checking.

"I'm forty-eight," he said.

"That's not too old."

"I'll be forty-nine next month."

"You could live another thirty years, easy."

"Not in this body."

"Your body's fine. I like your body."

"If I fucked you, I'd only be fucking her," he said, and he turned to the wall, his back fluffy with hair.

"I'm not her," I said.

"You're all her."

I got up and went to the bathroom and washed my face, my hands, everything already clean. The soap had flecks of oatmeal in it, like tiny bits of paper and insect wings. I filled a coffee mug with water and drank it and then I stood still and listened.

AUNT JEMIMA'S
OLD-FASHIONED PANCAKES

At lunch I sit in the ditch with the thin popular girls and pretend to be one of them.

Kitty passes around a bag of grapes. I take a couple and peel the skin off with my teeth, roll the wet balls around in my palm. Kitty is beautiful and rich but it's not the life she wanted. She has an eating disorder. Everyone wants to fuck her. Everyone wanting to fuck you is not as good as it sounds. I'm an artist, she tells me, when there's no one around to remind her what she is, but today is Friday so she's a cheerleader: legs shaved all the way up, red bloomers on over her panties.

Kitty doesn't like my boyfriend. She tells me I can do better. She says I'm funny and smart and pretty and he's in band, she says, *band*. So what if he plays drums. So what? So I write him a note in Chemistry and tell him it isn't working out. Then I watch the bones in his hand shift as his pencil moves over the paper.

He folds the note back up and passes it to the Gong girl who passes it to Allie who passes it to me. I put it in my purse, sandwiched between two pads.

On the way out, Dr. Cobb gives me the finger.

"You should sign up for the astronomy club," he says. "You could really use the extra credit." He puts his hand on the small of my back and presses like he can turn me off and on. "There's so much to explore out there," he says, dreamily. He slips the sign-up sheet in front of me and I sign my name and pay my dues but I don't intend on seeing any stars.

At home, I fix a sandwich and eat it in front of the television. The phone rings. It's my ex-boyfriend.

"I'm in the middle of something," I say.

"Like what?"

"Like a sandwich."

"Fuck your sandwich." I listen to him breathe and then he says, "Leann. Leann, Leann, Leann," and I say, "Julian. Julian, Julian, Julian," and he hangs up because he has to go to band practice. I know where he goes, who he talks to, what he wears, so there's really no point.

I change into my jeans and spray some perfume into the air and walk through. Then I watch TV until Allie picks me up.

We sit in front of the cheerleaders. Kitty does back handsprings every time we put points on the board and by halftime we're up by fourteen. We always win. I imagine it feels a lot like losing. My ex-boyfriend files out onto the field with his drums suspended from his neck, and then the band starts up and then they stop and the drum line screams something into the sky, something about Aunt Jemima, and it used to embarrass me, the absurdity of it, how people would ask me what they were saying and I never knew because I'd always forget to ask him and then it would be the next Friday night before I was reminded of it again.

I spend the night at Kitty's. Her mother is in the kitchen, heating up leftovers for us, when we get there. It's late and she's wearing her tennis skirt. I want to let her hug me because I don't have a mother and I need whatever love mothers are willing to part with, but we go upstairs without saying hello. "I'm kind of hungry," I say. Kitty shuts the door behind us. "In a minute," she says. "I want to show you something." She takes her paintings from under the bed, stacked and dusty, and makes me go through them, same as she does every time I stay over. The new one is of a top-less blonde woman on a beach chair. Her eyes are closed and she looks like she might be pregnant. Her towel has tiny hula girls all over it. There is nothing particularly sad about the painting but the colors are faded blues and greens and there is what appears to be a bruise on the woman's leg.

"It's good," I say. It's great, actually, but I don't tell her this. Despite evidence to the contrary, it is still hard for me to believe she feels pain. We listen to Kitty's mother make her way to her bedroom and then we go back downstairs and the food is on the table, steamed vegetables and a couple of chicken breasts. At my house, there would be bacon left over from breakfast and I'd make a BLT. I'd use white bread and a thin layer of mayonnaise.

After we finish eating we put on our pajamas and get in bed and have what she calls a deep talk. We sleep with her cat, Fatty, between us and the next morning my ex-boyfriend calls while we're eating our Grape-Nuts and I tell him he can't be calling me all the time, that we can be friends at school but that's it.

"You're such a bitch," he says.

"What's in your mouth?"

"Waffle," he says, which reminds me of Aunt Jemima so I ask him and he tells me it's Aunt Jemima's old fashioned pancakes and I don't ask why, though that's my question. I tell him it sounds delicious. Kitty looks up from her bowl.

I have a license but no car. Kitty has a car but no license. My father has a car I could borrow but something's wrong with the air suspension so it bounces like a Mexican's every time you hit a pothole, and he has a truck, but it's a stick and I can't drive a stick. Already three boys have tried to teach me and with each one there was the hope that maybe he'd be the one I would learn for.

She asks her dad if I can drive her BMW. He's staring out the window in his suit.

"Sure," he says. He shakes my hand and slaps my back like he just sold me a set of knives.

"Thanks a million, Bob," she says.

I tell him I'll be extra careful, but he's already out the window again.

I adjust the mirrors, turn the windshield wipers on and off, but I get lost on my legs, how skinny they are, how a person can shrink to almost nothing with so little effort. Two spins around the block every morning and a diet built around cereal.

"What are you doing? Let's go. You've got me on child-lock. That one, on the door, press it."

"I'm familiarizing myself. You're supposed to familiarize yourself in an unfamiliar vehicle," I say. She throws her hands in the air like go on then, get it over with why don't you?

"Your dad lets you call him Bob?"

"He's hard of hearing."

I crack the sunroof, turn on the air conditioner. "Okay, I'm familiar now. Where are we going?"

"Nowhere."

"Which way is that?"

"Any way."

I drive by her boyfriend's house, honk. "Move," she says. I step on the gas.

She seems disappointed. Her boyfriend, Jet, is in the grade above us. He's bad but he never gets in trouble because he's good-looking and his father owns a chain of grocery stores. Sometimes she drags me along on their dates and I ride in the back while he tells us how to pass a drug test, or explains the law of supply and demand. He talks to us like we're not even there, like he's working stuff out in his head.

I pull into Fast Lane and we go in and buy handfuls of Laffy Taffy. I'd rather have a Kit Kat but Laffy Taffy doesn't have any fat.

"Where do you find a dog with no legs?" she says, reading the wrapper.

"I don't know."

"Right where you left him."

We drive by my ex-boyfriend's house. The light's on in his bedroom and it makes me want to press my hand to the window but I don't because I don't want Kitty to see my hand pressed to the window. It reminds me of the time I went with my dad to Vicksburg and we ate at this nice restaurant and then I sat in the coffee shop while he played slots and I kept reading the same paragraph over and over because I couldn't stop watching him rub his hand over the screen. It made me sad, how much he wanted something he would never have.

We stop at Allie's and Kitty runs in and fishes her out. She arranges herself on the hump in the backseat. "I look like shit," she says. "Where are we going?"

"Nowhere," I tell her.

We drive by Allie's boyfriend's house. "I don't feel like talking to him, I just saw him, like, twenty minutes ago." He's in his driveway, washing his car. I pull in behind it. "Good going," she says. "Great." He drops the hose and climbs in the backseat and now it's four of us and I'm in charge. I don't like being in charge. I shove a grape Laffy Taffy in my mouth and step on the gas. Every time I check my rearview mirror, I catch his eye.

"Your head's in the way," I tell him, readjusting.

I drive by the mall.

"Next you'll take us to Starbucks," Kitty says.

I take them to Starbucks, park, but no one gets out. So I back up and drive through other parking lots, dozens of them, one connected to another.

"Less pavement, please," Kitty says. I take the frontage road to the interstate, go north.

"Is there a strip mall out this way?" she says.

"We're going to the country."

"Where's the country?"

"Outside the city."

"You're contrary," she tells me, pressing her toes to the windshield. "I have cute feet," she says. "Look at them. The pinkies are such tiny niblets." I agree that the pinkies are tiny niblets. Allie and her boyfriend are quiet, his head in her lap, her fingers strumming his hair, his ribs, the pockets of his shorts. One road leads to another, leads to another, and we're on gravel.

"Where are we?" Allie says.

"My dad's land, there's a trailer. It's in the middle of nowhere. There's a beaver lake."

"I've always wanted a beaver lake," Allie's boyfriend says.

"My dad wants to blow it up. They're eating up all his acreage. He used to take me hunting out here. He'd put me in a tree stand and tell me to keep still and I'd sit there and wish I had a brother and seeds or some shit would fall on my head and I'd watch my dad get smaller and smaller and then a lifetime would pass and I'd watch him get bigger and bigger and we'd walk back through the woods and I'd be sure we were going in a circle but then we'd see the truck, like a miracle, and he'd take me to IHOP so the next Saturday morning I'd get up and do it all over again."

"You were such a fat kid," Kitty says.

I pull up to the trailer and look through my key ring, four keys, one of them I never use, this one. I put it in the lock and open the door and turn on the light: a couch, a table, a row of bottles lined up on the counter next to the kind of toaster that only makes toast, and a coffee pot. My father keeps saying he's going to take away my key because he doesn't want me to bring my friends out here to get drunk, and he doesn't want me to bring boys out here because he knows boys, he was once, a long time ago, a boy.

Allie's boyfriend sits on the couch and she sits with him and they resume plucking at each other. Kitty and I sit at the table and then she walks over to the counter and picks up each of the bottles and reads their labels before putting them back down. "We could get drunk," she says, and everyone agrees that we could get drunk, that it's a possibility.

"It'd be fun to spend the night out here," Allie's boyfriend says.

"No A/C, bugs," I say.

"We could get fucked up and look at the stars."

"No one looks at stars."

"Didn't you just join the astronomy club?" Kitty says.

"I was coerced."

"Are there any board games?" Allie asks. Kitty and I look at her. Allie isn't our smartest friend. When she writes me notes, she uses a lot of exclamation points and puts commas in places commas don't go. A comma is a pause, I tell her. You don't want people to be pausing everywhere. Her boyfriend's hand moves over her leg, back and forth, back and forth. Kitty looks at me. "Where are our boys?" I think about my boy, how he's probably at home playing Grand Theft Auto, picking up prostitutes and kicking the shit out of people. He never even tries to collect whatever it is that needs collecting so he can move up.

"I hate you."

She stands behind me and puts her arms around my neck. "You love me," she says, and my muscles tense and hers tense in response but she doesn't let go. I breathe in her hair; it's a smell I know but can't locate. It's not coconuts and it's not almonds but it's something like that, hazelnuts, maybe, if I could remember what hazelnuts smelled like. And then we turn to watch Allie's boyfriend pour whiskey in a cup.

"Okay, I've got a game," he says. "I'll take a sip and pass it to the next person and they'll take a sip and pass it to the next person and we'll all hope no one has mono." He raises his eyebrows and drinks. His Adam's apple bobs. "See how fun it is?" He hands the cup to Allie and she sniffs it and says she likes wine coolers, she likes daiquiris. She sticks her tongue in and takes it back out.

"It's nasty," she says.

"Drink it, you pussy," her boyfriend says.

"It's not nice to call your girlfriend a pussy," I say, and I remind myself that I can say whatever I want because I'm very thin. It pops into my head like a life raft. Go look at yourself, it says. Make sure you're still very thin. Find something narrow and slide through.

"Drink it," Kitty says.

Allie takes a sip and turns her bottom lip inside out. I kick her under the table and she passes me the cup. I think about the wine at church and how they say no one ever catches anything but it still seems unsanitary.

I pass it to Kitty. She takes a mouthful and Allie's boyfriend says, "That's how it's done, girls, watch and learn, watch and learn." I roll my eyes. The cup starts over and soon it's empty but it gets refilled and we go outside and sit on two steps like we're taking a picture. Kitty passes around a pack of Marlboro Lights and we all take one, blow smoke.

"Is this cigarette stale?" I ask.

"You always ask me that," Kitty says.

She hides them in a potted plant in her backyard. When her parents are gone we sit out there on a couple of flat rocks and smoke and I watch her to make sure she's inhaling.

We wait for it to get dark and then we don't know what we're waiting for. Bugs toss themselves against the porch light. Clink, clink, clink. Allie's boyfriend points out the North Star. He says it doesn't move so you can use it as a guide. "Everything else moves," he says. My thoughts scatter. I put my fingers in Kitty's hair, braid and unbraid the same piece until she yells I'm pulling it out. She gathers it up and moves it to one side but I can't stop myself from touching it. It's shiny and soft even though she blow-dries it every day. She stands and goes inside and I remember a time when I wasn't Kitty's friend, last year, how I had a bad haircut and wore clothes that didn't fit, how I passed my Friday nights on the couch eating pizza and watching movies with Julian. Now, she says, I can have anyone I want but boys still look at me with the same eyes they looked at me with before.

Allie and her boyfriend stand and walk off and I know they're going to find someplace to have sex, and I think about my ex-boyfriend, how he writes me songs on his guitar and how these songs have details I hadn't noticed him noticing, like the mole on the bottom of my foot, which he called a freckle because you can't write a song about a mole, and the birthmark on my thigh, how he could live forever on that tiny island and be happy. I never even had to fuck him.

Kitty comes back out and sits next to me and we're not drinking because no one is around to see us not drinking and neither of us likes to drink—the taste, the way it makes us feel out of control. It's something we admitted during one of our deep talks.

"I wish there was a Taco Bell like right there," she says, pointing into the dark. "I want a Mexican pizza." I know she knows exactly how many calories are in a Mexican pizza, and that she'd work out until she burned the whole thing off, even if it took all night. Sometimes she loses it and eats a box of donuts and we can't hang out because she has to run sprints the rest of the day.

"I miss Julian."

"He isn't good enough for you," she says.

"What does that even mean, *good enough*?"

She rakes her fingers through her hair, leans back and moves her head from side to side to make sure she's collected every strand and then wraps it up in a bun on top of her head. Immediately it starts to come loose and I help it along: I yank and it falls. *Cascades.* She touches her head and looks at me and touches her head again in disbelief. I feel a few strands laced between my fingers like a spider web. I turn my face to her. Slap me, I think. Slap me. I want her to do it. I would put my hand where hers had been and feel the warmth creep to the surface. She doesn't do anything but stand and go inside and all of a sudden I'm scared. I don't know why I brought them here. The one time my father and I spent the night in the trailer I couldn't sleep. I stayed up all night trying to separate the noises that belonged from the ones that didn't, but all of the noises were unfamiliar so everything was in question. I was sure, for example, that I heard a man right outside the door taking the longest piss in history, and I was also sure that when he finished relieving himself he would come for me.

I watch Allie and her boyfriend walk across the field.

"We're leaving," I say, and I go inside and start looking around, making sure things are turned off and unplugged, even things I know we didn't touch. I turn off the porch light and lock the door and we get in the car. I drive too fast. I take a wrong turn and get turned around. Allie says I'm scaring her and Allie's boyfriend says I'm a racecar driver and Kitty doesn't say anything. She presses her feet to the windshield.

I make Allie get out at her boyfriend's house and then drive the short distance to Kitty's, park next to her mother's Lexus. My dad used to have a Lexus but he sold it, along with his fishing boat and one of his Four Wheelers. I stood in the carport and watched men talk him down, handfuls of cash.

Her mother and father are sitting side by side on the couch, watching television. She takes the keys from me and hangs them up and we go up to her bedroom.

"I'm going to call my dad," I say. She gets in bed and turns on the television. I call my father and he comes, honking once from the driveway. I see Mr. Maloan on my way out. He's in a white t-shirt, eating a bowl of cereal. He was once a boy, I think, riding his bicycle and playing baseball, getting into trouble.

"Thanks for letting me drive Kitty's car."

He looks at me like he doesn't know who I am. Other times he knows exactly who I am—he asks how my father is doing and takes the back roads to my house—and it used to hurt my feelings but it doesn't anymore because it's clear there is something wrong with him, with their family.

"Have a good night," he says.

I take my bag out to the car. It's so old it has my name painted in bubble letters and a yellow balloon.

"I'm sorry for waking you," I say, and he pats my leg: pat, pat. My father goes to sleep when it gets dark. I don't sleep well. I used to let it bother me but now I don't—I read or I walk around the house and look at the shapes things take in the dark.

"Is there anything to eat?"

"Rotisserie chicken and ham. I went to the store. I'll grill you a ham and cheese when we get home."

I sit at the table and watch him take the bread and ham and cheese and butter and mayonnaise from the refrigerator. He puts a jar of pickles on the table and I eat a spear while sorting through this morning's paper. I read the horoscopes and advice columns, check to see if I missed anything good on TV.

He delivers my plate and waits for me to take a bite and say it's good and then he says he's going hunting in the morning and goes back to his bed-room and I sit there eating pickles. Pickles have five calories per spear. Ham and cheese on white bread with mayonnaise and butter have more calories than my head can count. I'm not good at math. My ex-boyfriend is. In Chemistry, he reads novels about the apocalypse and Dr. Cobb doesn't say anything because he's so far ahead of every-one he doesn't even have to follow whereas I miss one step and that one step snowballs.

I put my sandwich in a baggie and stick it in

the refrigerator behind the gallon of milk so my father won't see it. Then I do my bedtime rituals same as I always do them and get in bed. I close my eyes but I just lie there and think and then I get up and roam around the house. I move from window to window, looking out, until my eyes start to make things up. I'm quiet even though there's no reason for it—my father can sleep through anything—but I keep waiting for him to stumble out of his bedroom in his underwear with his gun cocked, how I'd stand there calmly and say *don't shoot* after pausing a few beats too long.

TEMP

I spend my weekdays stuffing envelopes and answering the telephones for a financial company. I'm always disconnecting people and jamming machines, giving myself paper cuts. It's something about an easy job that makes it hard. During breaks, I talk to this guy named Jason who works nights as a bouncer. Come up to the club, he says. Bring a girlfriend. I'll let y'all in for free, hook you up with some drink tickets.

Jason wears the same three shirts. He has a body that reminds me of a jellybean and he smokes like a fag. I'm not attracted to him but I like the way he sees me. He calls me the hot young temp, as in, Hey, it's the hot young temp. And then one day we're sitting in the break room and he looks at me and says, You're a nervous girl, you know that? You're always playing with your hair and touching your face. It's your hands. They don't seem to know what to do with themselves. Things are uncomfortable after this even though he apologizes and brings me donuts and coffee every morning for a week.

A big girl named Karen sits next to me. She wears matching outfits in primary colors and has a large flesh-colored mole on her cheek. She doesn't have much use for me. I suspect it's because I'm the hot young temp. I suspect she hasn't noticed that I pull out my hair. Karen has an oral fixation. She hums or else she's got something in her mouth. I never say anything, but I look at her sometimes and smile and she smiles back but it's a quick nasty smile.

Karen tunes her radio to the Christian music station. When I look over, her eyes are closed tight and she's swaying. One of her fat hands is in the air, blessing some imaginary something. I take this opportunity to stare at the mole. It's like cookie dough. I want to squeeze it, see how long it can retain its shape.

Her cubicle is decorated with pictures of her nieces and nephews, birthday and holiday cards, a plant, two ceramic angels, and the clock radio. I've been here six weeks but there's nothing personal on my desk. I don't want to make myself at home in a place like this, with people like this.

My phone starts ringing at eight-thirty on the nose and I'm saying, Good morning, LNS Financial. How may I help you? over and over again. It's like sawing off an arm. I accidentally disconnect a hostile man. I suck in air, put my fingers in my mouth and say, Oh shit. Karen says, *Language*, in a singsong voice. The man calls right back, and I say, I'm sorry about that sir, one moment please, and push hold. I suspend him there because I don't know what to do with him. The person he wants isn't in and he refuses to leave a message. I don't take messages, I transfer people, but no one seems to understand this. To appease him, I push hold again and say, Okay sir, go ahead with your message. The message is for a guy named Bob. I don't know a Bob. The hostile man tells me that Bob will know what it's all about, and he leaves three numbers where he can be reached but I don't write any of them down.

You really shouldn't take messages, Karen says.

I slip off my heels and rub my feet back and forth against the rough carpet, check the different times on all the clocks.

Babs brings her baby in after lunch. It's a pink shrimp of unknown sex she calls Cam. She holds it up and makes it do a little dance for Karen, who claps excitedly. It looks precariously held together. I wouldn't be surprised to see an arm or a leg fall off. I'd like to know how often it needs to be fed and touched, how often it shits and cries, but I just smile and say, What a great baby. They look at me, surprised.

Babs is the receptionist. She's on maternity leave, but she'll be back soon and then I'll go someplace else.

When I get home, Warren's on the couch. The television and lights are off. He looks up at me. His eyebrows shrink and expand.

How many? I ask.

I don't know. I didn't count.

Only drunks don't count. Everyone else counts.

It's a problem, he says.

I turn on all the lights and preheat the oven. Then I sit with him, with the idea of making something bad worse.

Twelve days. You only made it twelve days.

The longest twelve days of my life, he says, an eternity. He lays his head in my lap but I don't want it there. It's heavy. The room is spinning, he says. Make it stop.

I can't help you, I say.

The two of us together can't even keep small animals alive. Snakes, hamsters, two cats and one dog, all buried in the backyard under crosses made of sticks and shoelaces, though the dog was in bad shape to begin with because I selected the most rundown-looking dog at the pound. He was old and mangy with a bad hip but his eyes are what got me. They said: I'm fucked, but you can save me.

My boss at LNS Financial is a pear-shaped woman with tight white curls. The sour old cow is what I call her. She's loud and opinionated and she doesn't seem to know how unattractive she is, which bothers me for some reason.

On Tuesday morning, she hands me five hundred envelopes to stuff.

I need them by lunch, she says. They have to go out this afternoon.

I'm all over it, I say, because you can say things like this when you're impermanent.

While I work, Karen tells me about the blind date she had on Saturday night. It's just the two of us up front and we talk a lot. She's better than a wall, I've decided, and she must feel the same way about me. Plus, when you dislike someone, there's no obligation to listen or retain information. She tells me he's a neurologist or a nephrologist—whichever is the kidney—divorced, one kid, and a full head of hair.

Get to the good part, I say. Did you get any?

A lady never tells, she sings. Then she turns her Christian music back up and the fat hand starts waving again.

I get up and go to the break room where Jason's reading the newspaper. He doesn't see me and then he does.

Watch out, it's the hot young temp, he says. He puts his paper down and looks at me expectantly.

Stop it, I say.

Stop what? he says. You're gorgeous. He goes back to his paper. I sit at the other end of the table and dig the book from my purse, the bottom full of sandy cookie crumbs. I try to read but I can't concentrate. I look at him—already he has forgotten me. I touch my hair to see what it's doing, finger the small prickly spot I've plucked bald. He looks up and I put my hand down. He smiles and goes back to his paper and I walk behind him to the vending machine, insert a quarter and two dimes and my honeyroasted peanuts fall.

I go back to my desk and finish the last of the envelopes, deliver them to the sour old cow. After that the phones are quiet and I have nothing to do so I do nothing—page through magazines, push the cuticles back from my nails. Karen also has nothing to do but she's trying to fool me. She thinks she has to set a good example because she's been here for years and she has a plant on her desk.

He squeezed my breast, she says. I can still feel his hand there.

So the nephrologist felt you up, I say.

She looks at the ceiling and makes a small sound like she's going to cry which makes my heart break a little but then it feels whole again, impenetrable.

What happened?

Well—he walked me to my door and he squeezed my breast and said, *'I'll call you.'*

That's terrible. I bet he winked, too.

No, I don't think he did.

He's a jerk. Don't take his calls, I say, though I doubt that this will be a bridge she'll have to cross. Then I hear her mumble, *the cocksucker*, and I look at her and she looks at me and we see each other as if for the first time.

I have the urge to tell her about the first time I had sex, how the dick's ghost was left when the dick itself was gone, how I waited in bed for three days for it to go away and told everyone I had the flu. But instead I ask her if she has any chocolate and she pulls her candy drawer out wide and says, Have at it.

Warren's not home and there's no note. He leaves a note when he goes to the store or for a run so I know he's out drinking, probably at the Dutch Bar talking to men more than twice his age, men who discuss their purple hearts and piles. I take a load of laundry down to the basement. Then I make myself a sandwich but I just look at it. It's ham on white bread in the middle of a dinner plate. There's no cheese in this house, not even a loose slice of that orange square cheese.

I drink a beer and then another and then I get out the phonebook and look up Jason's number. I run my finger across the page and check it for ink. I want to call him because he said I was gorgeous, because when I drink I get desperate for something to happen. But he's not home. He's at work, at the club.

Well, well, well, if it isn't the hot young temp, he says. He's wearing a shirt I don't recognize and he's smoking in that hurried, effeminate way of his. He looks the same, but different. I'm wearing ankle boots and a skirt that hits mid-thigh. I could pass for a hooker. So you've finally decided to give me a chance.

No, I just felt like drinking and I'm broke, I say, and I smile and cock my head like a dog trying to decipher human speech.

He hands me a twenty dollar bill and says, No drink tickets on Tuesday. You know you picked the worst possible night of the week to come up here. Ladies night is tomorrow.

I can't take your money.

When somebody offers you something you

smile and say thank you, he says. I take it. He holds the door open and I go in and sit at the bar. When the bartender delivers my beer I try to look pleasant because I want to tell him all my problems, but he crosses his arms and turns his face to the television. I watch it with him for a minute. Then I walk back to the door expecting him to yell I can't take my beer outside but he doesn't.

What time do you get off? I ask.

Why? You want to see my house?

I have my own house, I say, though it doesn't feel like mine. I don't think it'll ever feel like mine because it was my mother's first. When she died she left it to me—there was nowhere else for it to go. She had a lot of things I wasn't allowed to touch and I still don't touch them. I don't even look at them. I grab his arm and go back in and take my seat and the bartender looks like he's ready to listen now but I'm too busy thinking about my dead mother and my alcoholic boyfriend and my temporary jobs filled with temporary people, but I'm not really sad about it. I only want to make myself cry.

I'm at six beers, one shot of whiskey, and four bummed cigarettes when he stands behind me with a hand on my shoulder. I'm in no condition to do much of anything but fuck.

Are you my prom date, or are we taking a picture for the church directory? I ask.

Cute, he says, the church directory.

I should get home. I have someone who might be waiting for me there.

Sounds promising.

He just got out of rehab for the second time in nine months, I say, and he nods and looks away because he doesn't want to hear about my boyfriend. And then we're in his truck and Dolly Parton is begging Jolene not to take her man. I ask him if he listens to country music, though the station was programmed, and then I ask him if he has sheets on his bed. Yes and yes, he tells me. Country music and sheets.

Are they clean?

Fairly clean.

Is fairly clean like not really clean at all?

Fairly clean is not really clean and not really dirty. Look—I can change my sheets. It's not a problem.

You don't have any diseases you need to tell me about, do you? I say, and he says he's disease-free, which reminds me of a personal ad: *disease-free smoker enjoys lifting weights, long walks on the beach, and movies starring Meg Ryan.*

I want to see his jellybean body so I make him take

off his clothes. It is altogether a bad idea. We're in his kitchen. His cat is rubbing itself back and forth against my leg while he stands naked under the spinning fan.

Don't do everything I tell you to do, I say. It's something I heard someone say once, perhaps on television, and I have been waiting for the opportunity to use it. He slips his jeans back on without his boxer shorts. Something's not right about you, he says, and this is how it goes when I show myself to someone who only knows me casually. They say, You're different. They say, You're fucked in the head.

He pours himself a glass of whiskey and we sit on the couch. He puts his feet on the coffee table, which isn't really a coffee table but an old trunk and watches television while I flip through his stack of men's magazines.

I've never gone out with a boy who reads these things. I bet you like go to all the hotspots they recommend and download pictures of Tara Reid and shit.

You're not going out with me, he says. And Tara Reid is over, by the way. Ever since she did that *Wild On* show.

I liked her in *The Big Lebowski*.

We ignore each other for an entire hour-long courtroom drama and then revisit the situation— he's sitting on one end of the couch and I'm on the other and the space between us seems like a very great distance to cross. I crawl across it to sink my teeth into his shoulder.

I'm taking you home now, he says, which makes me want to touch him, but he doesn't belong to me anymore. In his truck, I roll down the window and stick my arm out like I used to do when I was a kid. Make waves. The streetlights blink yellow, which means caution, which means nothing; no one is on the streets. When he pulls into my driveway, I don't get out. My boyfriend's car is still gone. Who knows when he'll be back? I look at my neighbor's house, an elderly woman whose husband is in the hospital. Probably she is watching me and wondering who this boy is, why I need so many, why I can't decide on one.

I'm not supposed to drink on this medication, I say, though I'm only on antibiotics to control my acne and the combination of the two don't do anything except make the medication less effective.

You're a bad drunk, he says. He has a toothpick in his mouth. He's rolling it back and forth between his teeth.

What's the point in being a good drunk? What's the point in being drunk if you have to act like you do when you're sober? I ask, and I grab the toothpick from his mouth and put it in mine. Then I pull him over to my side of the cab and straddle him because something about the taking of the toothpick changed things. And when he touches me, I think of fat innocent Karen, asleep in her bed with those pink foam curlers in her hair, how tomorrow she'll be sitting at her desk with her wide eyes wondering where I am.

Warren comes home late. The whir of the microwave followed by the smell of beef wakes me up. Let's do it doggy style, he says, climbing into bed on all fours.

You must be high, or an imposter.

I did have a couple of tall boys on the way home.

And a couple dozen before that, I'm sure.

Come on, he says.

You left the light on.

He goes back into the kitchen to retrieve his plate. He sits beside me, licking his fingers, wiping his mouth with the back of his hand. I feel nothing. You're breaking my heart, I think. This helps. You make a mean meatloaf, he says. The light, I say. He puts his plate on the nightstand and his fork clatters to the floor and then he turns to me, ready, and a part of me wants to let him so I can hate him for it, but another part of me knows it to be inadequate compensation. He pads back into the kitchen and fixes himself a glass of something and comes back and gets in bed. I take it from him and smell it.

What? he says. Three second delay.

Just checking.

It'd be good. You could ride me for hours.

No, thank you.

You're missing out.

I walk around to his side of the bed and pick up his fork while he watches me. I take his plate into the kitchen and rinse it off and put it in the dishwasher, turn out the light. Then I help him out of his pants and his shirt and his underwear. He likes to sleep naked. I like to sleep in a tank top and shorts and panties and sometimes I forget to take off my bra. I've always slept fully clothed, in the event of an unexpected event in the nighttime.

Baby? he says. I'm sorry.

It's okay.

I just like to drink.

I know.

You like to drink, too, he says.

I didn't say I didn't.

I know what you were thinking.

What was I thinking?

You were thinking I have a problem and you don't.

I wasn't thinking that.

I know you too well, he says.

Sometimes I say the same thing to him but I don't realize how threatening it sounds until he says it to me. *I know you too well. No you don't.* Let's go to sleep, I say, and he agrees but then he remembers his feet are muddy. He finds this hilarious. More often than not he's a happy drunk. More often than not I'm an unhappy drunk so who, really, has the problem?

I put him in the bathtub and kneel beside it like he's a child.

I played soccer, he says, in the rain. He takes the rubber duck and sets in the water. I always think about doing this but I never do. It has mildew on it.

The mud is deep in his toenails. I scrub them with the bar of soap and then with a washrag and then I declare him clean and help him out and dry him off and put him back in bed. I kiss him goodnight and he says he loves me more than anything in the whole world and I say I love him more than that even, which reminds me what I've done but I don't feel guilty. I only know I haven't gone far enough.

MY BROTHER IN CHRIST

"You're wearing Coco Chanel," he says to the girl at the bar. She was watching him. They all watch him. The pills he takes makes this pleasant, like he's a scuba diver and they're a school of fish.

"Yeah. How'd you know?"

"I know things."

The bartender sets a drink in front of him and he walks off without acknowledging her further. He's wearing black leather pants and a red t-shirt with a hole in the sleeve. She came to see his band play. He's the lead singer; he also plays guitar. And he can be counted on, at some point during the show, to lay down on stage and freak out like Marty McFly in *Back to the Future*, only people will love it. They will clap and whistle and he will jump into the crowd so the girls can pluck strands of his hair and put them in their mouths, swallow a piece of him.

She doesn't know where her friend is, is self-conscious all of a sudden, sitting here alone. She puts her purse on the bar and unzips it: keys, wallet, lipstick, an unopened pack of cigarettes, mirror. In the side pocket: tampons, cash and a single condom, though the condom is for emergency use only because it's so old. The foil package says it expired December of 2000.

The lead singer's name is Jeremy and she's known him for years because her brother is the drummer in his band, but it's his habit to pretend everyone is a stranger. Her brother, Avery, is backstage now, drinking scotch. Earlier, she drove him to Wal-Mart to buy laxatives and fiber supplements because he's always constipated. Then she took him to her apartment so he could see where she lived and she watched TV while he made long-distance telephone calls.

"Dana, what're you doing? I thought you were in the bathroom. Come on," Mel says. Mel takes her hand and guides her through the crush of people. She's beautiful, so girls get out of her way, and boys smile as they help her along, gently touch her shoulder as she passes.

Dana is attractive in a less reliable way, like if you were to ask one hundred people whether she's beautiful, maybe sixty of them would say that she is. With Mel, it would be more like ninety-eight. In a way, though, she thinks it's good to be less obvious because some days she likes to be invisible and watch the world pass without interfering.

Jeremy's on stage, saying, "Test one, two,

test one, two," into the microphone. He's staring at her. It feels like the devil collecting her soul, but she doesn't look away. Avery comes on stage followed by the bass player, Sean. Dana used to sleep with Sean, but Avery didn't like her fucking his friends, so she stopped and their relationship is much better now. He doesn't call her a whore anymore, or tell her that their father is turning over in his grave, which she hated because their father isn't even in a grave. He's in an urn. She's not sure where because her mother moves him around. Sometimes he's sunning himself at the kitchen window, other times he's the centerpiece on the dining room table. For a while he was in the attic. That was right after he died and Dana put him there because her mother was cursing him to hell, which she considered unwise seeing as he killed himself.

Avery raises his drumsticks at her and smiles. He's kind like this sometimes, in the space between drunk and sober.

"We're Jilted," Jeremy says quietly and steps away from the mike, and then Avery taps his drumsticks together and says, "One, two, three, four," and they start playing. Before they were Jilted, they were Stood Up, and before that they were Classic Yellow. The name Classic Yellow came from a bottle of French's mustard, but its origin as their original band name is unclear as everyone blames someone else. Dana thinks it was Avery. She remembers him eating a hotdog at the kitchen sink, reading the bottle of mustard like it was a cereal box, but this could be one of her false memories. She has a tendency to rewrite things even as they're happening, to create stories in order to fill in gaps.

"I'd screw him on stage and they could call it the encore," Mel says. She's talking about Jeremy. The last time the band was in town, Mel got trashed and showed him her tits when they were partying at the crappy motel where the band always stays. Then she stuck her tongue in her cheek and asked him into the bathroom, but he declined, and when she finally passed out, he told everyone she had chest hair.

Jeremy is one of the two percent of people who could give a shit about Mel.

"You're such a slut," Dana says.

"And you're not?

"I'm reformed. I haven't had sex in months," Dana says, and then they don't talk because they're dancing, only it's more like jumping rope because there isn't any room to move. A couple of fraternity guys are behind them and the fat one is smoking and Dana is afraid he'll burn her because cigarettes have a way of finding her arms like footballs find her head.

After the show, the five of them walk back to the band's room at the Moroccan Motel, which is in the same parking lot as the club. It's convenient this way because everyone, except Dana, is drunk or high. Dana used to sleep around and drink until she blacked out, but she's trying to be better. She's started going to church on Sundays and in bed at night she repeats *my body is a temple* until the words lose their meaning, at which point she moves on to *the meek shall inherit the earth*. She knows Mel won't inherit anything and this pleases her. And when she's horny, she tells herself that men are just her *brothers in Christ*. Sometimes it works. Sometimes she tricks her vagina and her head into believing these things, but mostly, it doesn't do any good because by morning she's forgotten that her body is a temple and she fills it with Pop Tarts, and then she forgets to be meek because she can never remember exactly what *meek* means.

Jeremy's on top of the covers, watching a porno. Two eighties-era brunettes are doing it and one of them is pretending to climax. There's a man's hard penis in the corner of the screen and a hand stroking it. Dana sits at a faux-wood table, chipping the polish from her nails.

"You know there's semen and puke and God-knows-what on that bedspread," she says, because she can't think of anything else to say and she wants to say something. Mel, Avery and Sean walked to the gas station to get beer. It's just the two of them.

"I'm sure I'll add to it by morning," he says, changing the channel. "You probably don't want to watch that."

In her head she's repeating *Jeremy is my brother in Christ.*

"There's nothing on. Do you mind, watching it? Surely you've been exposed to this kind of thing before."

The cherry falls from his cigarette. It lands on the carpet and she gets up and steps on it, pretends it's a spider that refuses to die. When he looks up at her, she says, "Your cherry."

"Sit," he says, without moving, and she says she's fine where she is because it was an unexpected offer and her first inclination is always to decline. She turns around and walks back to her chair.

"Why don't you like Mel?" she says.

"She's nothing special. Why do you ask?"

"I find her almost painful to look at sometimes, she's so pretty."

"I find you painful to look at," he says. On television, the prettier brunette is fucking the other one with the biggest dildo she has ever seen. Her mouth is open to accuse him of lying when the others walk in, cued by a director somewhere eager to move the script forward.

"My new puppy has a chip in her head so she can't get lost. I guess it's, like, hooked up to a satellite or something. How weird is that? Someday we'll all have chips and we won't be able to get lost anymore," Mel says.

Mel is always buying puppies or having her nose pierced or taking drugs because life bores her, and she talks constantly about nothing, or she has a way of making everything sound like nothing. This is why Dana hangs out with her—she never has to do or say much of anything herself, and they've been friends since the second grade, so it doesn't really seem like something she can get out of.

Sean is asleep on the floor. Dana studies his face. It looks different when he's still, less attractive. His cheeks are acne-scarred, his upper lip almost nonexistent. Avery's been in the bathroom for the last fifteen minutes, and Dana, Mel and Jeremy are sitting Indian-style on the bed, playing Go Fish, but they're not really into it. It's hard to get into Go Fish. The porno is still on, but the sound is off. It's two guys and a girl now. The girl has a bad bleach job and one small eye like Barbara Walters. She's getting fucked up the ass and doesn't look very happy about it, but if the sound were on she'd probably be saying, *oh yeah, right there, that's the spot, baby*. Dana heard somewhere that it's always the less attractive girls who get stuck doing anal.

"Do you believe in God?" Dana asks Jeremy.

"Absolutely. God almighty," Mel says, and then she asks Dana if she has any threes.

"I'm agnostic," he says, which she suspected. She thinks this probably makes it impossible for him to be her brother in Christ. He gets up to get another beer and Dana tells Mel to go fish.

"Why are we even playing this?" Mel asks. "It blows."

"Let's just play High-Low," Jeremy says, handing them each a beer. He takes a card from Mel's hand and lays it on the bed. "High or low?" he asks Dana. It's a ten, so she says, low, of course, but the next card he pulls is a Jack so she has to drink. High-Low is like Go Fish, with rules impossible to mess up or forget.

Dana's on the toilet peeing, her thighs pressed together, when he opens the door. She doesn't mind. She left it open a crack. She asks him to turn around so she can wipe, then pulls up her jeans and washes her hands in the bathtub, dries them on a scratchy towel. He gets them a couple of beers from the sink and sets the ashtray on the toilet. Everyone else is asleep.

Jeremy talks about his mother, about how she used to beat him and his younger brother. He says it went on until a few years ago, when his dad bought her a farm and a couple of horses to distract her. Dana thinks sometimes pain is nowhere to be found and other times it's all that seems to exist: Avery's sadness, their father reduced to ash and fragments of bone, Jeremy getting the shit kicked out of him by a society lady.

"You always act like you're in a movie, like everything you say and do has been edited and choreographed. You take too many pills. That's your problem," she says.

"How do you know?"

"I know things."

She removes the cigarette from his lips and takes a drag, puts it back.

"I'm just an asshole," he says, placing a hand on her thigh. He squeezes her faded skin. She doesn't go to the tanning bed like Mel and her other friends. Maybe she should fix herself up more, she thinks. Get some highlights and a manicure along with her Hawaiian tan.

"Do you want me?" she asks. It's a rhetorical question. She wants him to undress her without speaking another word, to leave a hickey or a bruise somewhere so she'll have proof, but he just

MY BROTHER IN CHRIST 159

lays his other hand on her other thigh. She takes a sip and sets the can back on the toilet, says, "This is a mighty fine establishment you've got here."

"Only the best for you."

He flips over then and puts his head in her lap; his legs dangle in the bathtub.

"I'm a lousy lay when I'm wasted." He traces her jaw line with a finger, touches her clavicle. "You don't want me anyway. I'm dirty."

She doesn't know if he means needs a shower dirty or what. She doesn't ask. After a few minutes, he's asleep. She runs her fingers through his hair, collects a loose strand. Then she puts the root between her teeth and swallows.

BIG WORLD

My father did not like my sister's orange hair.

He knocked once, pointlessly, on the window and said, I guess I just like things the way they're supposed to be, which made us laugh. How was anything supposed to be? The three of us were in the living room, trying not to look at each other. I got up and called my ex-husband to let him know I was in the state. How long? he asked. I'm leaving tomorrow, I said. The whole point was to let him know he'd miss me. I went back into the living room and took my seat. The stereo was playing at an irritatingly low level like the music was in my head.

My sister and I were home for our uncle's funeral. He had been nice to us growing up, unlike the rest of them, who didn't believe we would ever be anything but small. Before he died, he heard bells. The priest said it was God calling him home. I thought about the day before when I'd taken my trash into the alley and a homeless man looked right at me and said, I'll take that, and I gave it to

him and he said, thank you, which undid everything that had been so carefully done inside me.

The small dog pushed her bear into the middle of the room and started humping it.

What's she doing? I asked. What I meant was
why. She was fixed. She never humped anything.
My sister answered without thinking. I coughed;
she fingered a buttonhole on her sweater. We re-
located to the den where there was a focal point,
the television. My father wanted to watch the
news but it had been preempted by the weather-
man talking about an unhealthy line of storms.
Unhealthy was good, he assured us. He drew
squares around the bad areas, which were lit up
red, and the whole thing was very soothing, the
needless repetition, how slow he thought we were.
My father was angry. I want to hear what nigger
shot what nigger, he said.

Nothing we did could change his behav-
ior. If we loved him more or shunned him, if we
laughed at his comments or ignored them altogether. We discussed the situation endlessly and
with a certain amount of satisfaction, a problem
that couldn't be solved and therefore required no
solution.

After dinner, I took off my dress and hung it up,
the only thing in the closet. Then I got in bed. It

was my old bed. It had a canopy. There was a pile of stuffed animals in one corner of the room I couldn't bring myself to throw away. One day my children might want them.

I got out of bed and selected one to put between my knees while I slept.

Jackie stood in the doorway and said she was going out.

With who? I asked.

A boy, she said, you don't know him.

Is he a nice boy?

He's not in love with me, she said, which was confusing as a response but I knew what she meant: he was nice but he would only ever be so nice to her. I told her to be careful and to call me if she needed me to pick her up. She never called. She kept standing there so I told her I loved her.

I love you, too, she said. I didn't know why boys didn't love her.

The big dog got in bed with me and circled twice before lying down. I petted her awhile and then I touched her nose—pebbled leather, crayon black. She jumped off and jangled down the stairs. I thought about the things I'd said to people at the funeral, and the careful things people had said to me, and I thought about how special I'd felt sitting in the reserved section with the velvet rope, how the woman behind me touched my shoulder and I wasn't sad at all. At lunch, the other people who weren't sad and I said this to each other: It just hasn't hit me yet. We drank red wine and caught ourselves laughing. When everyone was leaving, my cousin Louise and I went outside to smoke. We were the same age but I didn't like her because she talked about hair products and shoes and whether the boyfriend she'd had for three months was going to ask her to marry him. They were in love, she said, and the sex was incredible. With every boyfriend it had been the same. You want it too much, I told her. You want it so much no one's ever going to give it to you. We were tipsy and someone was dead and I was under the impression we could be honest.

I called my ex-husband. I called him out of habit. I called him because there was no one else. I don't know if you ever met my Uncle Richard? I said. He died.

Rick? Of course I know Rick, we stayed at his cabin that time and a couple of Thanksgivings—.

I forgot.

—we went to their house. That sucks, he said. *Man. Rick.* I can't believe it.

Are you mowing the lawn?

Next door—the chinchilla. I've been cooking out.

Are you drunk?

I've had a few, he said, cocky now.

I have to go to the bathroom, I said, and

hung up. I didn't love him anymore. If you were a needle lost in a haystack, I'd told him once, I'd search until I found you, I'd search forever, but I was tired now.

When I woke up, it was still nighttime and my sister was sitting on the bed in the dent our mother had made.

I threw up, she said.

I'm sorry.

She crawled over me and got under the covers; we sank into the middle.

Were you having fun, before you threw up?

I never have fun anymore, she said.

Yes you do.

No, I don't. I'm nervous all the time. I didn't say anything. I was nervous, too. I recalled the fruit flies at work, how I hadn't noticed them until a coworker pointed them out. A car passed slowly, its shadow tracing the walls, followed by the security car with its blinking lights. The security asshole never caught anything as it was happening, my father said, he had no idea what they were paying him for, but it made me feel safe.

The next day it was just my father and I at the breakfast table. He'd made biscuits and sausage and grits and scrambled eggs. We ate while reading the newspaper, the dogs underfoot.

Wake your sister up, he said. Y'all need to get on the road.

We were thinking we might stay another day. She said she could call in sick.

They'll fire her.

They don't fire you for calling in sick one day, dad.

It's not a good idea, he said.

He went into the small bathroom and shut the door and locked it. I drank the last of my coffee and listened to him make noises that seemed impossibly loud, louder than if there'd been no door at all. I scraped my leftovers into the dogs' bowls and went upstairs.

Jackie had all the covers piled on top of her and she was sweating. I touched her shoulder. She didn't move. I got in the shower.

When I came back, she was sitting up in bed. She showed me her hands, how puffy they were.

What's the plan? she said.

Dad doesn't want you to call in sick. He says they'll fire you.

Did you tell him I'd slept with all the managers? Tell him that, she said. I could claim sexual harassment if they tried anything.

You should stop sleeping with everybody.

One of them I didn't, just two of them.

Don't tell me. I don't want to know.

I don't do that anymore, she said. I love myself now. I think I'm great.

You are great.

I know.

You're very special.

That's what mom used to say, she said. I made an exaggerated sad face but she wasn't looking. I wonder if she knows, she said. She probably doesn't even know.

She took a shower while I played with the small dog. I threw the golf ball and she'd bring it back but she didn't want to give it to me unless I acted like I didn't want it. Then she'd drop it at my feet and bark. She was always escaping and my father would have to go out into the neighborhood and call *treat* in a high voice, the treat voice, until she came running down the middle of the street with her ears blown back.

We hated to leave him, we told each other, but we were glad he had the dogs to keep him company. Otherwise, what would he do? He'd die. He'd be dead. We talked about him from the time we got on the interstate until we stopped for gas outside Canton. While I pumped, Jackie went inside to get a Diet Coke and came back with a thirty-two ounce beer.

Great, you're going to have to pee every twenty minutes now.

No I won't. My bladder is better than yours.

Best bladder, I said, you win.

She had her big sunglasses on, scanning stations. There were only country stations in the middle of nowhere.

Just turn it off, I said.

I'm bored.

So read a book.

I don't read, she said. She looked out the window—dead cars and animals and skinny pine trees—and said it was making her sick. I remembered how she used to have to sit up front, sandwiched between mom and dad, while I rode in the back by myself.

I think I'm going to get on antidepressants, she said.

Why don't you just quit drinking?

I don't know what I'd do if I quit drinking. I'd have all this time on my hands.

You could take up needlepoint or collage.

Fuck off. And I'd be lonely. I wouldn't have any friends.

Your friends are the kind who like company on their way down, I said, thinking we were all this kind. Have you ever tried to quit?

Once.

And how'd you feel?

Happy, she said. She smiled, remembering the way she imagined this happiness felt.

It was ten o'clock when I dropped her off at her apartment. Then I drove straight to the house of the guy I was fucking.

He answered the door in his bathrobe. He had eyes the color of a baby's—dead gray, undecided. He had brightly colored tattoos on his arms and thin hair pulled back in a ponytail. He was a card-carrying atheist, he liked to say, and it bothered me that he could be so certain about something so uncertain, but more so that he used the term card-carrying for something there was no card for.

I followed him into his kitchen.

I had to go out of town, I said. My uncle died. My mother's brother.

I'm sorry to hear that, he said. I opened his refrigerator and poured myself a glass of lemonade like I belonged there. I was about to take a shower and get in bed, he said. I wasn't used to being the one in this position. It was like a science experiment I already knew the outcome of.

My mother's missing. I don't know if I told you that.

Missing?

Like we don't know where she is.

Can adults be missing?

Anyone can be missing if there's someone to miss them.

I suppose that's true, he said.

She's not on a milk carton or anything. He took a sip of my lemonade and said it wasn't cold. He'd just made it. I looked at the wall behind him. What's that sound? I said.

What sound?

It's like somebody's doing Shake N' Bake in your wall.

The bug man came earlier, he said, so it's probably something dying. He opened his robe. He was hard and I hadn't even had to do anything.

I wonder what it is.

What's it matter?

It sounds like a rattlesnake. Are there rattlesnakes in Tennessee? I pushed his hands away. I didn't like for someone to undress me. I liked to undress myself. He picked me up and set me on the counter like a new appliance—where could he place me that I would be convenient, yet out of the way?

We looked at each other. I remembered the times it had been a completely different kind of challenge. He kissed me. Are you a whore? he said. Tell me what a whore you are.

I'm a whore, I said. I'm such a whore. I didn't believe it. Not enough to turn me on.

Tell me your fantasy, he said.

You already know.

Tell me again, he said, I like to hear it, so I

told him. It sounded like someone reading the directions to a test. He picked me up and set me down on the floor, rearranged me there. I looked at the wall. The thing was still rattling away. He put his hands around my neck—whore, he said, slut—and squeezed. Every time, things went further and further and I stuck around, wanting to see where things could go when there didn't seem like anyplace left.

He pulled out and came in my mouth. I could have spit but every time I had swallowed. A precedent had been set.

I left in a hurry like I had something to say about it. On the way home I called my ex-husband. I'm a vegetarian now, I told him. You don't know me anymore, I was saying. You have no idea.

That's stupid, he said. Why?

Because animals feel pain, too, I said. I didn't really have a reason. It had been a rash decision made primarily to prove I could make them. I was weak. My sister was weak, my mother, my father. I like animals, I went on, and I never really cared much for meat anyway. Just the thought of biting into a chicken leg—

I'm going to have to eat twice as much meat now to cancel you out, he said.

Are you seeing anybody? I asked.

No, are you? You probably have lots of boyfriends.

Just one, I said. He likes to choke me while
we're doing it. I liked to say things to shock him,
the truth. Like my father, he had sent me out into
the big world all alone and I was going to show
him how ugly it was.

F<small>ULL</small>

I'm at my cousin's house, watching her fix dinner for her twins, who are trying to toss themselves out of their highchairs. When I take care of them, my only goal is to keep them alive but I don't bother with them now because Courtney's here and if they crack their heads open it's all on her.

She cuts the hot dog lengthwise and chops it up like a tomato. Then she opens a can of green beans and fishes out the stalks with her fingers.

The phone rings. I answer it. It's her husband, Wade. He thinks I'm Courtney and I don't correct him. He says he's on his way home, he's running a little late, he's sorry. I hear an ambulance in the background. "There's a bad wreck," he says, and then he tells me he loves me. I hang up.

"He's on his way."

She points to a basket of laundry. "Would you mind folding those towels while you're just sitting there?"

"Let me finish my drink first."

I have no intention of folding her towels.

I have enough trouble folding my own towels. I watch her flit about and remember the reason I came over here. I figure the best way to get information about her people is to insult one of mine. "My sister *never* returns my phone calls. She's such a bitch," I say, and I remember the time my sister screwed her over, the stink that followed.

"She just doesn't think sometimes," she says diplomatically.

"Only about herself."

She twists her red hair into a pile on top of her head and sits down. We look at the twins, squishing bits of hot dog in their fists, waxing beans into their trays. She gives them a stern look and says, "Eat." They look like all babies: bigheaded and big-eyed and pale, nothing special.

"So tell me about Erin's new husband. Do you like him?" I ask. I heard no one likes him and it isn't just because he installs sewer systems for a living. He's been in trouble, my mother told me, but she wouldn't say what for. People don't tell me anything because I have a big mouth.

"Well—," she says, stalling. "I promised Erin I wouldn't talk about it, but he has a rap sheet."

"Like what, he got busted for pot or something?"

"No, more like statutory rape of a thirteen-year-old girl. Of course he swears up and down he didn't do it. Up and down. But still, these are the kind of people he hangs around—trash. But then he's trash, too. He wears these big gold chains and you should see his chest hair." She makes her hand a claw and holds it between her breasts to show me what this looks like.

I say, "Gold chains are terrible," and she looks at me like *no shit*.

Her dog comes over and sticks his nose in my crotch. I push his head away but he keeps coming back because I have my period and I remember the time she told me she was trusting her tampon. This was before the slogan, Trust Is Tampax. We were smoking behind the movie theater and waiting for her mother to pick us up in her station wagon.

"Mustang, get offa her," she says.

"He's okay."

"Just kick him, if you want. I don't think these kids are hungry."

We look at the food they've thrown all over the floor and shake our heads. I'm glad I don't have to clean it up. I don't know what I'd do if I had to clean up hot dog and shit all day long.

The garage door opens, closes. Wade comes in. He kisses his wife, his children, slaps his dog and says, "Good boy," before turning to me. "Was that you on the phone?" I smile. He wags his finger.

Wade is getting fat, but I still want to sleep

with him, and I think he wants to sleep with me, too. Of course I think nearly everyone wants to sleep with me. I don't know why this is. Maybe everyone thinks this way, or I'm nuts. Courtney is mean to him. She talks to him in a voice reserved only for him because he's a doctor but he doesn't make as much money as she expected him to make. She tells me, there are rich doctors and there are poor doctors, but they live in a big house and she drives a nice car so I don't know what she's complaining about.

Wade sits down and I ask him if he wants a glass of wine.

"That'd be great."

I pour him one and top mine off. Courtney doesn't drink, except on special occasions, and this isn't one of them. It is one more reason to hate her.

She tells Wade to clean the kitchen and he says, "Can I rest for two seconds, please?" and she says, "I don't care what you do. Rest forever," and takes the babies upstairs, one on each hip. She has already lost the baby weight. She likes for her wallet to match her purse to match her shoes to match her outfit.

We wait a moment for the air to clear.

"How was your day?" I ask.

"It was bad and then I came home," he says. He works with a kind of incurable cancer and it gets him down. When Courtney's sick, he avoids her. He can't even prescribe my birth control pills. I always imagined doctors could fix things, but now I know that some doctors fix nothing. And all day long, people asking for things they can't deliver.

"I'm sorry," I say.

"Don't be."

"I feel like going somewhere."

"Like where?" he asks.

"Oh I don't know. Out to dinner maybe, or Madagascar."

"Madagascar?"

"I've been reading this blog and the girl's in Madagascar right now. She's trying to join this club where you have to set foot in a hundred countries in order to belong. I like how it has all these words built in: mad, gas, car."

"I hadn't thought about that," he says.

The dog rests his head on my leg and I feed him a potato chip.

"I have my period," I say, running my scissor fingers over his soft ears. I am always announcing my period to everybody. My mother says if I didn't say anything no one would know, but I can't help it. I know.

"I'm sorry."

"It hurts."

"Did you take something?"

"Not yet."

"You should take something," he says. "Courtney wants to go to Cancun. She sent off for this catalogue that lists all these resorts and they all look alike but she still managed to pick out the most expensive one." I want to tell him Courtney is wrong for him, but they have a house and two kids and wedding photos hanging everywhere and maybe if I had these things with him it would be the same: I'd be bitchy and the children would be awful and spoiled, the house dirty. At night, I'd have to beg him for it.

"Pretty water."

"I can't think of anywhere I want to go less."

"So where do you want to go?"

"Alaska." He looks up at the ceiling and blinks.

"I hear it's a good place to find a man," I say, and I think of my boyfriend, his olive skin and hazel eyes, and how, nine months ago he changed the song on his MySpace page to *Don't You (Forget About Me)* and that's how I knew he was dead. I got his furniture and his things, since they were already in our apartment, and I still live among them, but when people look at me now they don't think: her boyfriend killed himself, or maybe they still do. I don't know. I should move.

"Not your type," he says.

"I'd find me a big ole rugged man and we'd

live in a cabin he built with his own two hands."

"You'd get tired of cabin living."

"You don't know."

"You aren't really the rough-it kind. You're more of a room service girl, like my wife."

"No offense but I'm nothing like you're wife," I say. I let that soak in for a minute and then I tell him that I'd find me a big ole rugged man who liked to watch meteor showers and write poetry and drink wine and he wishes me luck.

"Don't be so negative," I say.

"I'm just kidding. I'm sure you could find a sensitive poet who builds cabins in his spare time and only drinks merlot."

"That's what I've been trying to tell you," I say, and I smile and he smiles and we get stuck there until he gets up and uncorks another bottle. I thread my fingers through the dog's hair, past the scratchy top layer to the soft undercoat.

"He's shedding pretty bad right now," he says. I pull my hand out and look at it, covered in stiff black hairs. I turn it over slowly, like that scene in *Back to the Future* where Michael J. Fox is disappearing. "I need to w-a-l-k him."

Mustang barks.

"Uh oh," I say.

"Do you want to come?"

"I don't know. Can I bring my drink?"

"If you want," he says, but I know he doesn't

want me to. Their neighborhood is full of rich people keeping up appearances. God is big, as are fences and dogs and babies. I don't have a house or a fence or a dog or a baby and God and I are currently on a break. I think about that picture with the two sets of footprints in the sand and how there's only one set during the worst times because that's when God carries you but what good is being carried if you don't realize you're being carried, if you get to the end of your life and have to ask?

"I told Courtney I'd fold these towels," I say, because I just want to sit here with him a little while longer, because I know he won't leave, but then the babies start crying. We look up at the empty stairs.

"Bath time," he says.

"Fun."

"Barrels."

"They're such sweet boys. Do you love them a lot?"

"Sometimes I love them so much. It's overwhelming."

"What about the other times?"

He shrugs. "You can't walk around all the time feeling like your heart's going to burst."

The water cuts off. I set my purse in my lap, soft black leather, full. Inside, my boyfriend's wallet, exactly as he left it minus five large bills and six small ones, which I gave away to a homeless man. I look through it when I have to wait somewhere, read the business cards and flip through the pictures of his sister and his mother, eighteen-year-old me.

"I better go," I say, but I don't move. It's like a boulder, pressing me down, and I remember how, when I first started carrying a purse, it was empty so I filled it with things I didn't need, to take up space.

ANIMAL BITE

I sat across from a crumpled woman who appeared to be miscarrying. A man stood over her, his hands on his hips, his head, everywhere but her. I examined the back of him, the ass shifting in his jeans, the occupied loops and wedge of hair, while a Mexican family sat in a corner watching television and a black girl leaned against a water cooler. I asked if she had a dog. From what I'd seen, black people had no use for dogs.

"No," she said. "My dad ran over it and said it ran away."

"How do you know?" I asked.

She looked like she wanted to tell me it was complicated but then she told me she found it all messed up and her chin started to wobble.

I removed the wad of paper towel from my face to show her the split between my nose and lip, in a place I had no name for. My husband, Ed, squeezed my leg and I put it back. He was older than me by nine years, had gray hairs mixed in with the black. When I suggested he pluck them, or dye them, he always said the same thing: I'd rather they turn color than turn loose. He had a handful of phrases like this that made up his entire personality.

Someone called my name and I went and sat in a chair and a fat lady asked what happened.

"A dog bit me," I said.

"Whose dog was it?"

"My dog."

This seemed to please her. She took a form from a cubbyhole marked ANIMAL BITE and started checking things off. "Rate your pain on a scale of one to ten with one being no pain at all and ten being the worst pain you ever felt in your life," she said. She pointed at a chart on the wall in case I needed help. The faces with no pain looked happy and earlier, before my dog bit the shit out of me, I wasn't in pain but I wasn't happy, either. It was misleading, the idea that lack of pain equaled happiness. I said I was a two or three but I'd been drinking. It was Saturday night, weren't normal people drinking? I wasn't going to feel bad about myself for it.

She led me to a room and my husband followed. He sat on the chair and I sat on the bed and then he walked over and stood next to me and I took his finger. I could see my head in his pupil. It was so small. Sometimes he pretended to pluck it off and throw it far away, other times he plucked it off and took a bite, tossed it over his shoulder like a bad apple.

A nurse with enormous pores came in, asked what happened.

"My asshole dog bit me," I said.

"Is that a new breed?" she said, bending over me to examine it. I looked into her pores and thought of water swirling down a drain, that little spinning tornado.

She left and came back with a needle. I unzipped my sweatshirt and pulled out my arm and she stuck me.

"Does it hurt?" she asked.

"No."

"Mine hurt the next day," she said.

"Well you can call me tomorrow if you really want to know," I said. She didn't say anything to that.

The doctor was thin, her blonde hair in a messy ponytail. I preferred less attractive doctors. She had to go into another room to get smaller gloves and then she came back and pulled the wound open from either side. "Dog bites are nasty," she said, "and we usually don't stitch them because they get infected easily, but I'm going to stitch this one because it's on your face. It should heal up rather nicely." She just stood there with her arms at her sides so I showed her the scars on my stomach and legs, told her I had the kind of skin that didn't heal up nicely. I wanted her to ask where the scars came from but she didn't. I wanted her to say I had a pretty face.

She numbed it up with nervous hands. Then she came at me with a blue sheet of paper with a donut cut out and I tried to put my head through, but she said, "No, not like that. It's so you don't have to watch me stitching you up."

She poked at me with the needle and asked if I could feel it. I said I could. She asked if it hurt and I said not too bad so she began and it didn't seem like she was doing anything I couldn't do at home.

After she was finished, I stared at the ceiling and remembered my horoscope from that morning. It said I should expect a windfall. I didn't know where a windfall might come from. I didn't have a lottery ticket or rich relatives, and my husband made a lot of money but I never saw any of it because he was cheap. Our mattress was so old you could feel the springs but he wouldn't buy a new one even though he woke up every morning complaining about his back.

"You okay?" he asked.

"When can we go?"

"Shouldn't be much longer."

"They just leave you sitting in here forever," I said.

"Just try and relax."

"I'm getting rid of that dog."

"No skin off my back," he said. It was another of his sayings. He hadn't wanted a dog in the first place, I just brought him home from the Animal Rescue League one day and he seemed like a normal dog until we gave him a pork chop and he snarled and lunged at my foot when I went into the kitchen for a glass of water.

"It's never any skin off your back," I said.

"Hey—," he said, like I should be nice to him. He was in the middle of the football game when the dog bit me, was in his underwear, had been drinking.

The nurse came back in, freshly powdered. The powder sat on top of her face but soon it would sink into her pores and amplify them further. Soon it would look like a landmine and if you looked closely there would be tiny appendages everywhere. I pictured myself on her face, collecting soldier's arms and legs, perfect except for what was missing.

When we got home, the game was over. He couldn't find the score so he had to call his brother. His team lost. His team always lost. I told him he should just pick another team, one that didn't suck, but he said that was the dumbest thing he'd ever heard. "You can't just pick a new team," he explained, "you're born into a team." It was a question of loyalty, of tradition. He called the town where the school was located The Land of Milk and Honey and a few times a year we went there, stood in the stands and got drunk and then fretted about how we'd get home.

I sat with him while he watched recaps of teams he wasn't born into. His team never even made the recaps. They were always throwing turnovers, had no offense to speak of. I had learned some of the lingo, against my will, after so many years.

"If they always won, it'd probably feel the same as losing," I said. I had been on losing teams and it wasn't that bad. I recalled my swim team: a group of large-breasted girls who drank milkshakes and asked each other if our tampon strings were hanging out. Before meets, we'd pass around packets of Kool-Aid like real swimmers.

"You need to pipe it," he said. I opened my mouth and he said, "Pipe—," and I closed it. It was a game we played.

I went to the window and looked out. The dog was down there, looking up at me, looking down at him. His eyes were swirling and empty, as if he'd been hypnotized.

Earlier, while Ed was watching the game, I sat next to the dog and put my head in his space. He was curled up on the guest bed, a black-and-white ball on the white comforter. He opened one eye and groaned and I should have left him alone but I kept on harassing him because I was drunk, because I wanted to see if the dog and the husband and the house and the job were things I could extricate myself from, one by one, without making myself look too bad. No one would blame me for getting rid of a food-aggressive dog that bit me in the face. Even the vet said I'd gotten a bad one, that some dogs were born unsalvageable, like some people.

"Should I let him in?" I asked.

"Hell, no."

"He's never slept outside before."

"He's a dog," he said. "Dogs are animals. Animals sleep outside. Come sit down."

I sat. The couch cost $65 at the Salvation Army. Flowers on an off-white background, it had probably belonged to an old lady. I imagined her house full of quiet punctuated by ticking clocks, her husband already in the ground. My side was dirty from my feet. Grubby, he said, grubby grub worm. He used it as the reason we wouldn't be getting a new one anytime soon.

He pulled at his t-shirt so I scratched his back, my hand making a large circle around the kite string of moles below his left shoulder. They were bumpy, the kind that bled easily. I didn't have moles but I had freckles. You could scratch right over them. I made a few rounds and then told him I was going to bed and he turned off the television. We always went to bed at the same time even though he was a morning person and I was a night person. It was something we'd started and it seemed too late to stop.

I brushed my teeth while he peed and then we traded places. We ran our mouthpieces under the faucet and carried them into the bedroom. I'd begun grinding my teeth shortly after we met. He'd given me other things I'd never considered before, like these little bubbles on the rims of my eyes. They appeared overnight. In the morning I scraped them off with my fingernail.

He propped up on one elbow to look at me.

"Does it hurt?" he asked.

"No. I'm still a little drunk," I said. "We shouldn't drink so much. Why do we have to get drunk all the time?"

"We won't drink this week," he said, which was what he always said, but we usually couldn't hold out past Wednesday. Hump Day, he called it. On Hump Day, he'd come home with a twelve-pack of beer or a fifth of whiskey and we'd drink and drink and I wouldn't have to think about any of the things I usually thought about, like whether we were happy, or whether we'd ever have a baby. And I wouldn't think about the stack of folders waiting in my inbox at work, and how as soon as I whittled the stack down the pop-eyed Wanda would come and fill it back up and I'd want to kill her even though she was nice and had some intestinal disease and she was just doing her job. And I wouldn't think about the time I wasted in the mailroom, pretending to look for something while I imagined the young, white manager coming up behind me, his dick on my ass as I reached for something high. It had happened once before, a couple of years earlier, a mistake, he'd said. I wasn't in love with the young, white manager. We had nothing in common besides being young and white but standards were lower at work, where, like pot lunches, you had to make do with what was offered.

My husband put a hand on my forehead. He wasn't a bad guy; we just weren't right for each other. Somewhere out there was a girl who loved chicken wings and football, a girl with her own set of clichés I was denying him.

"I feel like hurting myself," I said.

He had a gun. It was small, had belonged to his grandfather. Sometimes when he was gone, I took it out of the little box and turned it over in my hand. I thought about all the people who'd managed to pull the trigger and I knew I wouldn't be one of them. I would wait this thing out. I'd wait it out past the point of nothing to wait for.

"Don't be silly," he said.

"I could kill myself."

"You're being ridiculous now. It'll heal."

"It's not because of that."

"What's it because of then?" he said.

"I don't know."

I wanted to tell him I was leaving, but I knew if I left I'd just want to come back. We had a house and jobs with benefits and we had each other. I liked his family better than I liked mine. It was like that children's story my mother used to read to me, the one where the kid was going to run away but then he started packing up the things he had to take with him and it turned out he wanted to take everything, not only the cookies his mama baked but his mama, too. Otherwise, who would bake them? He piled it all high on his bed, and I thought of the things I'd pile on ours, how I would keep going and going until the bed finally gave way under the weight.

NOT ALL WHO WANDER ARE LOST

The first thing Norbert tells me is that he's been to all seven continents, including Antarctica. We're supposed to tell something about ourselves that no one would suspect along with the biographical info and this is Norbert's something. I can't think of anything, so I tell him I'm a horrible waitress, though I probably look like I'd be a horrible waitress. I tell him I am easily overwhelmed.

Norbert sits one row to my left and one seat back. The class is called Planning and Managing Learning and the teacher is a gay man with a small body and a large head. Norbert and I often get paired together by default because I'm antisocial and he's a know-it-all. I call him Hobart by mistake. People have been screwing up my name since birth, he tells me. I'm sick and tired of answering to Hubert and Nordstrom, he says.

Getting involved with Norbert outside of class is accidental. I'm at the sandwich shop across from my apartment complex and so is he. It's a Tuesday. We're both alone. Standing there with our sandwiches, it seems impolite not to eat them together.

Norbert has no desire to go back to Antarctica. Too goddamned cold. He has four kids around my age. He's divorced. He had a vasectomy in May of '94, which is when I graduated high school. He tells me all of this, and more, over sandwiches. Mine is turkey and Swiss. His is a brownish meat with circles of white fat dripping an orange sauce. A bit of the sauce falls on his shirt and he dips a napkin in my cup of ice water and rubs. His midsection is vast. The wet spot grows and grows. The whole thing is vulgar and more entertaining than a bad car wreck. Finally, he gives up and turns his attention to the crumbs at the bottom of his bag of chips. Then he goes to the counter and buys me a macadamia nut cookie. I'm allergic, but I don't mention it, just stick it in my purse and thank him. Tell him I'm stuffed but I look forward to eating it later.

The girl who sits in front of me always wears the same pair of jeans. In blue permanent marker down one thin thigh she has written, Not All Who Wander Are Lost. I think about this a lot. Not All Who Wander Are Lost. Her name is Beth. She has great hair and a tattoo on the back of her neck. She wanders but she is not lost. That's all I know.

Norbert taps me on the shoulder and asks to borrow a pen. Ever since he bought me a cookie, he acts like I am required to supply him with pens and sheets of paper. I make a mental note not to let him buy me anything ever again.

After class, he hands me his business card, tells me to call anytime. I say okay. His card says Norbert E. Pringle, Neighborhood Network Consultant. It has three different telephone numbers, a fax, and an email. I have no idea what a Neighborhood Network Consultant is but it sounds like a suspiciously inflated title. Driving home, I think about Waste Management Technicians, Sandwich Artists.

Norbert is like a red Explorer after you've just purchased a red Explorer: everywhere. I see him at the bookstore, at the grocery store, twice at the sandwich shop, once at the mall.

At the bookstore, Norbert tells me he was in the Navy. My favorite place was Italy, he says. I also liked New Zealand and Spain. I can tell he wants me to ask him questions about this former life, so I ask if he ever cheated on his wife with a hooker. He says he did, but he always felt bad about it afterward. That's no excuse, I say.

That's how it was back then, he says. Things were crazy. I give him a look. I lived with death on a daily basis, he tries. In my mind, hundreds of men in white uniforms and caps are jumping off a bridge. They're in a conga line. They all look like Norbert.

People like me should not wait tables. I never know who ordered what. I serve cold soup and neglect to offer dessert. I have sex with the manager, which tends to upset somebody. In this case, his girlfriend. It started one day when I cut my finger and I went to his office to get a Band-Aid. I sat on his desk and let my blood dirty his paperwork and he spread my legs. I forgot about the finger. His name is Arthur and he's a bad drunk, but he's good at some things.

I've quit twice but both times Arthur talked me into coming back. He goes to the trouble because I look good. Sometimes good-looking people really do get special treatment. Don't let them tell you they don't. He doesn't seem to care that I'm deathly afraid of the customers, that I spill things on them, that the only tables that tip me at all are the ones full of men in suits, men who drink scotch and forgive pretty girls anything.

I work five nights a week but it's not enough. My father pays my rent, which is five-hundred and fifty dollars a month, and sometimes he covers my cell phone as well. I'm twenty-nine years old. He told me I'd have to move home unless I went back to school and finished my teaching degree, got a real job. One that didn't require special no-slip shoes.

At the mall, Norbert is eating an ice cream cone in the food court. I'm shopping for jeans and thinking about Beth. How she wanders but isn't lost. How I'm lost but don't wander. How her hair isn't a single color but tiny sections of red and blond and brown, like each piece has its own area code. As always, he's by himself and so am I, which puts me in a bad spot. It's hard to decline an offer when you're alone. People assume you want company.

Norbert tells me to sit and don't move and I do as he says. He comes back with an ice cream cone for me; it's dipped in chocolate. I hand him a couple of dollars but he shakes his head. I say, take it, in my most demanding voice and he says, your money's no good here, like he's running a business.

When Norbert opens his mouth, I see the ice cream melt on his tongue, soft and white. He says, you're a special person, Kate. You're wrong, I say. I'm not special. It doesn't make me special. The *it* I'm referring to is my looks, though it's crass to even allude to your own beauty. It shocks and alienates people. Then Norbert gets a brain freeze. He puts his head in his hand and grunts. The other hand holds what's left of his cone. Goddamned brain-freeze, he says, coming out of it.

In class, I ask Beth what her tattoo says. It's the Chinese symbol for luck, she tells me, but so far it's for shit. I lean back. I'm disappointed because I was hoping it would be a clue of some kind. Something to add to the other. Her jeans are getting thin, holes everywhere. Soon, I know, the ass will start to go and when that happens, it's over.

Norbert needs a sheet of paper. Make that two, he says. I feel like writing you a love letter. I say, look, Hobart. You don't borrow a sheet of paper from a girl to write her a love letter. You use your own paper. Beth overhears the exchange and turns her head so I'm staring into her ear. Like her jeans, it's full of holes. I think I love you, I want to whisper in it. When she turns her head back to the teacher, I hand Norbert the two sheets he asked for and tell him to knock himself out.

After a dry spell, I run into Norbert at the bookstore. It's the week before Christmas. He's wearing a khaki trench coat and loafers but no socks, his spindly legs bare. When he sees me, he comes at me with his arms wide open and folds my body into his, plants a kiss on my cheek. You look like a flasher, I say. He smiles and takes my hand and we sit on the bench and watch CNN. Some nut's been shot on an airplane because he said there was a bomb in his carryon. You just can't do stuff like that anymore, Norbert says. Used to be you could do all sorts of crazy shit and no one would bat an eye. I know what you mean, I say, though I don't recall a time like this.

Well, I got back together with the ex, he says, and I say, yeah? That's great. And he says, no, not really. Something was wrong with the woman. She bled all the time and had to have all her female parts removed. That wasn't the reason it didn't work out, though. Didn't work out because it never worked out. We sit there for a while without speaking, and then he says, so tell me. What's been going on with you? and I shrug to indicate nothing. I'm still at the restaurant, I say. Still seeing someone. Like a counselor? he asks. No, like a man, I say, and he scrunches up his nose, revealing black shoots of hair.

The man I'm seeing is Arthur, who is still seeing his girlfriend Bee. The only thing that's changed is the amount of cartilage in Bee's nose. They're in Chicago right now visiting her family, but I don't tell Norbert this. I pretend my boyfriend is waiting for me somewhere with a glass of eggnog and a slice of nut bread. Nut bread, huh? he says. I love nut bread, and I smile and say, good to see you again, Hobart.

On Christmas Eve, Arthur walks around the restaurant with a mug of vodka, his shoulders slumped forward like he's been kicked in the gut. He sets his mug down next to my bowl of lemons and yawns. For the past month, he's been paying me twelve dollars an hour to slice lemons into flowers, but mostly I smoke or read or suck him off while he does paperwork. Earlier, when I was between his legs, he told me he wanted to kill himself, and I said, could you wait till I get your dick out of my mouth first?

Bee comes in after closing and sits at the bar. Billy the bartender sets a frilly drink in front of her and she smiles as she unravels her scarf. I'm also at the bar, also drinking something frilly in celebration of the season. There was nothing wrong with your nose before, I say. It's the most obvious nose job in history. Like a freaking ski slope. She goes back to Arthur's office and Billy stands in front of me with his arms crossed. You're such an ass, he says, and I say, yeah? So are you. Once, back when Billy was a waiter, he pointed out my bald spot when we were making out in a bathroom at a party. It's a wonder you ever get laid, I say, and he shoots an invisible basketball into an invisible net. Then he winks and says, score.

Several drinks later, I hear Bee come clackety clacking down the hall and then she shoves open the door and walks out. I watch the lobsters crawl on top each other for a while and then I walk back to Arthur's office and lie down on his desk. He pulls off my pants and then my panties and then he covers my vagina with his mouth. I barely feel a thing, but I moan because he likes it when I carry on. I think about the lobsters, the way they squeal when dropped in boiling water. When it's over, he smiles and says, Merry Christmas, angel.

Arthur tells me he only stays with Bee because she needs him. He tells me this after he gives me a gold star-shaped necklace and I give him a poker set. Let's not talk about it right now. I have another gift for you. It's a Christmas sweater, I say, holding it up, and he says, I see that. The sweater is the kind somebody's great aunt would wear: bright green with snowflakes and blinking lights. Just what I always wanted, he says. I hop up and down and say, put it on, put it on, and he slips it over his head and holds out his arms. What do you think? he asks, and I say, there's no way you can kill yourself in a sweater like that.

Later, we're in bed and it's quiet except for the sound of a train. I take a picture of Bee from his nightstand and study it. She's ice-skating, her dark hair in ringlets under a knit cap. The frame is silver with red hearts. I took it in Chicago, he says. She gave me the frame. Are you going to marry her? I ask, and he says, no. I'm not. There are things you don't know. I don't want there to be things I don't know, I say. I want to know everything. I straddle him and pin his arms to the bed, but then I just slide off and ruffle his hair.

In the morning, he gives me a stocking filled with chocolates and lace panties. You can keep those undies here, he says, and I say, like hell. Put your Christmas sweater back on, I tell him, and he groans and goes upstairs to get it. When he comes back down he pops a bottle of champagne and pours two glasses but I grab the bottle and take a swig. I'm wearing one of his button-down work shirts. I feel like a girl in a movie. Model your new panties for me, he says, and I stand in front of him, unbutton his shirt and slip out of my cotton panties that say Tuesday. Slip a pair of pink lace panties on. Turn around and show him my ass. Very nice, he says. No shit, I say, and then I look over my shoulder at him and smile as wide as my mouth will stretch.

I change into a skirt and blouse, and go over to my father's house.

A long time ago, I saw my father shoot up. He's a lawyer now, rich off asbestos, but I still picture him with a needle in his arm—face slack, eyelids violet, naked from the waist up.

I sit under his tree, which is massive and decorated with silver bows and delicate glass balls, and open my gifts. The big one is a laptop. The small one, diamond earrings. They're three quarter karats, he says, and I hold them up to the light before sticking them in my ears.

After lunch, I tell him I have to go. He says, you always have to go.

Something about him disturbs me. His cavernous house and tear-drop chandeliers. The way he stands with his hands in his pockets like he's trying to hide a boner. Everything around him seems phallic, and I'm not sure which one of us is the pervert.

Check out those sparklers, Arthur says, when I walk in. Good gosh. Maybe I should have gone with you. He gave me a computer, too, I say. No shit? he says. Makes my gifts look like crap.

I strip off my nice clothes, put his button-down back on. Then I take his hand and lead him into the bathroom. We spend a lot of time in the mirror. I monitor my mouth for lines, pluck my eyebrows, try on new shades of blush. He watches his hairline recede. Another one off the front lines, he says, holding up a fine hair between a thumb and index finger. Another fallen soldier, I say. He releases it, washes it down the drain.

In the kitchen, he opens the fridge and sets the eggnog on the counter, pulls the plastic ring from the top and pours me a glass. Here you go, he says, sliding it in front of me. Better drink up before it goes bad. It's fattening, I say. You made me buy it, he says. There are starving children in Africa, and the United States of America. I stick my tongue in and pull it out. Maybe we should call Bee to come over and drink it. She can spare the calories. He doesn't say anything, and then he says, you know the reason I stay with her? I stay with her because you wouldn't want me if I wasn't. He bows his head a bit. It makes me wish I was wearing a kimono. A blue one with flowers, peonies or black-eyed Susans.

Norbert's business card is tucked behind my license, and every time I go to pull it out, I'm reminded of him. I think about discarding it, or sticking it in the top drawer of my dresser so it can get lost in the mix of patient education pamphlets and other crap, but I don't. I think he'd be a good person to call if I ever had a flat tire, or if somebody put me in the hospital.

At the drugstore, when the girl cards me, I'm faced with Norbert and his Neighborhood and all of the numbers associated with his Network, and for some reason, this time, I get the urge to call him. I sit the box of Coronas in my passenger seat and listen to Dave Ramsey talk to some idiot woman about car repossession and wait for it to pass but it doesn't so I call his cell and tell him to meet me at the food court in the mall. He says, I'll be there in five minutes. Unattractive men work harder, I tell myself. They're more accommodating. But I don't want to fuck Norbert. I only want to watch his face light up at the sight of me.

Arthur's at home, waiting for me to deliver his beer. Also, I promised to fix him Mexican food. More exactly, I promised a Mexican fiesta, which means not only burritos but side dishes: refried beans and guacamole. Bee is out of the picture now, which makes me the girlfriend, which makes me responsible for such things. The care and feeding of Arthur. It hasn't been going well.

Norbert takes me in his arms. He squeezes once, hard, and releases. I say, hi, and scratch my head. I sniff like I have a cold. I feel like I should explain but he just says, have a seat. I'll get the ice cream. Dipped? You want yours dipped? and I say, please, and he goes over to the Dairy Queen counter and stands in line. I stare at his backside, at the way he bounces on the balls of his feet and looks around with a pleasant expression like a complete pervert.

We eat our cones and watch the post-Christmas traffic. Everyone is fat, some of them unbelievably so. I open my mouth to point this out but Norbert is also fat, not unbelievably fat but fat enough that you shouldn't mention other fat people. I close my mouth and watch him devour his ice cream and then he's popping the last inch of it in his mouth. That hit the spot, he says, and I say, yeah. I eat the chocolate off mine and lay it on a stack of napkins. Let it melt. He snatches looks at it while asking me questions: what classes I've got lined up for the spring semester, what I got for Christmas. Then he presents a small box. Now I'm gonna come clean here. I bought this for my daughter but I forgot to give it to her. It's all wrong for her, anyway. Norbert—, I say, and he says, you're gonna open it and you're gonna wear it. If you like it, that is. But I'm pretty sure you'll like it.

The bracelet is gold and has tiny charms on it, a tennis racket and a baby bottle and a saxophone, among other things that don't apply to me. I don't play tennis, I say, and he says, nobody'll be looking that close. It's gold. That's what they'll notice. I don't want it but I thank him and hold out my wrist, and it feels wrong because I never wear bracelets but I imagine this one breaking me in. I imagine becoming the kind of girl who wears bracelets and plays tennis.

I hate to run, I say, and he says, so don't, and I explain about the boyfriend, the beer in the passenger seat of my car. Perhaps if Norbert were younger or better looking, we might go sit out there and get drunk and take off our pants but that's not going to happen. I hug him and say goodbye, Hobart, and shake my ass as I walk through the sliding glass doors.

Arthur is on his feet when I come in. He's drunk and he wants to know what happened to his Mexican fiesta. When I speak he says, blah, blah, blah, and tosses his hands into the air. Fuck off, I say, and then I walk back out to my car and drive home, my phone ringing the whole way. It sings from the depths of my purse until I turn the sound off and then it hums. When I finally answer, he says, I can't do this anymore and I say, you haven't done much. What have you done? Then I hang up and wonder if this means I'm fired and I'm pretty sure it means I'm fired because he's the only reason I'm still there.

I walk the box of beer up the flight of steps and into my apartment. I have things to do: bills to consider, a fish tank to clean, clothes to wash. None of it pressing.

My father calls. He asks if I've hooked up my computer yet. I tell him I think I got fired and then I say, it's a laptop. There's no hooking anything up. He says, you know what I mean. Then he just sits there, breathing, and I'm reminded that breathing can be a challenge for some people. Why do you *think* you got fired? he asks, and I say, dad. You know I can't wait tables. I never *could* wait tables. I've been slicing lemons and making salad dressing for over a month. They're doing me a favor by keeping me. No, he says. You're doing them a favor. You're smart, and you're beautiful. Remember in high school, how you won all those awards? Yeah, I say, I remember, but I don't mention that the awards were for remedial classes, like Algebra 3, which didn't even exist, which they invented for those of us incapable of moving up to Calculus. I thank him and hang up. I am always thanking everybody.

I drink a beer and clean the fish tank and pray the fish don't die from shock like they usually do. A massive hole wells up inside me as I scrub. It reminds me of the time I stayed in my dorm room after everyone left for the holidays and I stared at a crumb of oatmeal for days. I considered removing it from my desk, but I couldn't, so then I just considered how lonely it looked, all alone, a crumb of fucking oatmeal, and I thought I would lose my mind. I quit not long after that. When it looks like the fish won't die, at least not right off, I go through my bills. It's something about going through them. You're not even really required to pay them after that.

Arthur shows up and I answer the door because I'm just sitting on the couch, holding my own hands. He apologizes and I accept and then I call us in a pizza. While I'm on the phone with the girl, he says, so much for my Mexican fiesta, but I pretend I don't hear him and he doesn't say anything else about it. For now, until I can find another one, I need this job. I don't want my father paying for everything with his asbestos money like he does for my brother in Los Angeles, who is trying to be an actor, who imagines he is the Next Big Thing.

We fool around but I'm not into it. He buries his head beneath my shirt and says, I'm a little ground hog, in a high voice, and then he says, your tits are unbelievable, in his normal one. He feeds me other compliments that bounce right off. After a while, the pizza comes. The pizza man's car is a lowered, neon green Honda Civic. I watch him walk back out to his car and stick one thick leg in and then the other, in a move that is akin to the limbo.

Arthur says, I'd eat but I'm too horny. I shrug and open the box, take out the slice with the most mushrooms. He puts his hands on his knees and hoists himself up with some difficulty. The implication is that he is tired, that he is tired of me.

He walks back to my bedroom and digs through my stash of porn (left over from a boyfriend who moved out West to find himself) while I watch from the door. I know which video he'll select. I just like to confirm that I could leave and return in five years and I wouldn't have missed a single fucking thing. Everyone likes to watch their own shit get worked on, he says, holding it up.

In the morning, it's all pass the sugar and would you mind making me some scrambled eggs? And, lemme help you with that. And then he notices my bracelet. Where'd you get this? he asks, holding my wrist. I found it at the park, I tell him. I never go to any park but it seems like something a person might find at one. You're an indoorsman, he says. You don't go to the park, and I say, you're wrong. I love parks. I love small animals and brisk walks and trees and flowers. I especially love flowers. I name every flower I can think of while he puts on his shoes and slings back the last of his coffee and walks out.

I'm scheduled to go into work at four. I don't know whether I still have a job but I don't have anything else to do and I need to pick up my min-iscule paycheck, so I put on my black pants and my black shoes and one of my father's old white shirts and drive to the restaurant, stopping along the way for a hamburger.

I try the door to the office but it's locked. Tim comes up behind me and says, Arthur's not feeling too well, says he's got heartburn or indigestion or you're killing him.

Since Arthur called in, Tim is in the kitchen tonight. He tells me to make salads and dressings and slice a shit-load of lemons and no smoking every five minutes or hanging out with the busboys. We're gonna be slammed, he says. There's a party of sixteen coming in at seven and another party of twelve coming in right after. Then he elbows me in the shoulder and smiles, walks off.

When I first started working at the restaurant, I took Tim to church, which I'm confused about now because I don't go to church anymore and he never did go to church but we went there, together, one Sunday morning, and then we went to a Chinese restaurant and ate mu shu pork and read each other's fortunes. Then he fingered me on the way home and everything fell apart. We've just recently gotten over the trauma of it.

I'm on my twelve-hundredth lemon when Tim says, so you ran her off, I hear, and I shrug, refocus. I'm getting really good at lemon flowers. You set one on top of a bed of lettuce and it's like a tiny perfect garden on your plate. Bee ran herself off, I say, and he says something that starts strong and then slides off a cliff. What? I say. Speak up, I can't hear you, and he says, you don't know what you want so you just take whatever comes along. I set the knife down and look at him, but then Billy comes into the kitchen and says the party of sixteen is here, and Tim rests a hand on my back, lets it sit there long enough to burn through my shirt, before moving down the line.

I finish the lemons and the salads and stack them in the small refrigerator. Then I walk around until I find Tim standing at the bar, talking to a regular. I'm finished, I say. So unless you want me to suck off your busboys, I'm outa here, and he says yeah okay, go on, and elbows me in the shoulder. I tell him to stop touching me and he says he just can't help himself. I can't blame you, I say. I'm *immensely* touchable. When he smiles, music starts playing, or a ray of sunshine breaks through the clouds, something awful like this. I say, see you tomorrow and he says, yeah okay, see ya tomorrow, and I say, bye and he says, later.

At home, a message from Arthur. He's sorry. For what he doesn't know. He's still thinking about it. It's not much of an apology, but he doesn't really owe me one. I feed my fish and talk to them, briefly, about what I think my situation is, but the fish seem to think I have it all wrong.

The next day, I shop for groceries and pay some of my older bills, the ones that were due before Christmas, so I won't get phone calls from Indians named Janice and Bill. Arthur calls a couple of times but I don't answer and then I find him at my door. He sits on my couch with a glass of water. I say, if we stop seeing each other, am I fired? because I don't really want to be fired, and he says, you're sort of pointless, you know, and his eyes narrow and fall in a way meant to take the sting out of such a statement. That's true. But maybe I could go back to waiting tables, I say, and he doesn't say anything so I talk myself out of it. Though I'd probably kill myself if I had to crack another lobster, and I still can't open a bottle of wine without fucking up a cork. Then he says, you can stick around until you find something else and I say that might take awhile and he says that's okay. He'd hate to see me go.

He doesn't say anything else about the bracelet, though it's still on my wrist, creating a ruckus. Clinking and clamoring with all its false allegations. My favorite is the house. It has a door and two windows and a chimney. It's the kind of house a child would draw, under a giant yellow sun, with an assortment of connected stick figures nearby and a tree with a giant afro. My second favorite is the key. The key holds the secret, I tell myself, or else it unlocks the door to that house.

After he leaves, I take a nap. Get up in time to go to work.

Tim says Arthur's not coming in. He says he's taking a few days, and I say, I just saw him, and he says, yeah well—. What'd you do to him? Nothing, I say. Then he shrugs and tells me I'm on desserts.

Typically, the waiters prepare their own desserts, coaxing ice cream out of massive containers, heating up pie, and decorating plates with swirls of chocolate and fans of strawberries. Desserts are hell. Already I miss lemons. I want to leave at nine, like I usually do, but I get the idea that I shouldn't ask to go home before the last dessert is served.

After closing, I sit at the bar with Tim and Billy and several of the waitresses. The waitresses don't talk to me for reasons having to do with I fuck everybody and get paid twelve dollars an hour to slice lemons. I drink beer. Tim drinks whiskey. Traci sits in between us drinking a Diet Coke because she's an alcoholic, which she's always bragging about.

Traci's hair is bleached white-blond and her nose is sloped like Bee's, only her nostrils could conceal walnuts, so it's probably real. Despite these things, she's beautiful, and I want to be her friend. I ask how she did tonight and she says, a hundred and twenty, and I say, that's really good, and she spins her stool around so I'm looking at the back of her head, at the little barrette in the center of her trashy hair. Tim was talking to Billy but then he stops and gives me a look that nearly breaks my heart. I finish my beer and go outside to the parking lot to smoke. I smoke one cigarette and then another and then I come back in to use the restroom, telling myself no one wants me here, that I'm a slut and an asshole, that I'm pointless and talentless and no one will ever really love me. On the toilet, I sit still and listen. I'm sort of horrified by the things I tell myself when I'm the only one around to hear them.

When I come back out, the girls are gone. Billy tells Tim that everyone's gone downtown. He says, meet us down there if you can, man, and Tim says, I don't know, man. I've got a ton of paperwork, and Billy says, yeah, okay, well if you can. Then Billy takes the Miller High Life cap from his back pocket and sticks it on his head. He tells me later and walks out.

We should meet them, I say, standing beside him with my arms crossed on the bar. I'm sure that would help your cause, he says, showing up with me. I don't have a cause, I say. Oh, that's right, I forgot. You're tough. You don't need anybody. Then he tells me to take a seat, and he gets up and goes behind the bar. Holds out his arms. What'll it be? How about a martini? I say, and he says, what kind, and I say I don't know what kind. Apple or strawberry or something fruity, and I want lots of cherries. No problem, he says. He tells me that he used to tend bar in Dallas when he lived there during college, and I say, I hear Texas is a nice state, and he says, you should go there. This one's too small for you. I've been meaning to tell you that.

Tim sets the drink in front of me and fixes himself another whiskey. I dip my fingers in and pull the cherries out, one at a time. Good drink, I say, and he says, good. He sits back down, and I turn my stool so my knees press into his leg. I've got stuff to do, he says. You can finish your drink. He stands and I pull him back down by the arm. You know Arthur can fire me, don't you? he asks, and I say, I'm aware. I can tell he wants to tell me what my problem is. His mouth opens and shuts and then it opens again and then he gets up and walks back to the office.

I watch the lobsters, tap on the glass to wake them up. I want to haul them out to the parking lot in the hammock of my shirt and set them free, maybe take a few pictures of the whole thing and call it an art project: lobsters crawling over pavement, gravel lodged in their carapaces, making their way to the interstate with tiny suitcases made of blue and green and yellow construction paper.

I knock on the door, push it open and stick my head in. What if I don't want to go home yet? I ask, and he says, you don't have to go home. Just let me finish this and I'll come back out. I wait a moment for him to look up but he doesn't.

We don't say much. Everything I want to say sounds wrong in my head. It sounds like begging. After another drink, he says, so what's going on with you and Arthur? I shrug. He wants me to cook and clean out his refrigerator and go to the liquor store. But I don't even clean out my own refrigerator and the only thing I know how to cook is Mexican food. Tim asks if I can boil an egg and I say, how come everybody always wants to know, *can you boil an egg?* Who even eats boiled eggs? Good point, he says. And then he says, poor people. I'm pretty sure poor people eat boiled eggs because they're cheap and full of protein. I want to tell him I was poor, that growing up my father was a drug addict and my mother was—I'm still not sure what my mother was—but I try not to talk about that, and when I do, to make myself feel better, I always mention that my father is rich now, that I stand to inherit a lot of money if he doesn't relapse and blow it all on drugs and hotel rooms and high-class hookers, but then I *really* hate myself. Poor people might eat boiled eggs, I say.

Do you think I'm pretty? I ask, and he says, of course I think you're pretty. You know you're pretty. Everyone knows you're pretty. It's hard to argue with everyone, I say, spitting the stem of a cherry onto the bar. I want him to undress me and lay me out on the floor, but then the bar begins to wobble and the lobsters fall asleep or die and something turns. Come on, he says. I'll walk you out. I give him my arm and he walks me out to my car like an old lady. If there's a moon up there, I don't see it. He opens my car door and says, drive careful. I watch him walk back into the restaurant. Call me when you get home so I'll know you made it, I say, before turning the radio on.

The next morning, I stay in bed and watch a miniseries on the Hallmark Channel. It's about a woman in the late nineteenth century who has two suitors: a rich man and a poor man. The rich man has land and fine china but he's stiff-looking and his speech is clipped and you can tell he would be a lousy lay, concerned with bodily fluids and such, while the poor man is square-chinned and passionate, but, of course, poor. No land, only the idea of cattle. With the poor one, she will die in childbirth from all that fucking or at the very least, grow old before her time. Even so, it's an obvious choice. The rich man is ahead and then he falls behind but then he comes back again and the poor man is sad, dejected. He visits his brother's grave and no one comes and lays a hand on his shoulder while he's kneeling there. I feel jerked around and manipulated but I like it, and then I think how the American public is made up of imbeciles and how I am one of them. Alas, the woman can't go through with it. When the rich man asks for her hand, she declines, sticks it to him with some crack about how he can't buy everything, and marries the poor one. I bawl and throw myself across the bed. I want to witness the deflowering but all I get is the two of them riding off in a covered wagon to some unknown impoverished destination.

Outside, snow falls but it doesn't stick. The phone is silent. I begin to think I need a cat: something else to avoid me, for me to avoid, only in close quarters.

Tim calls and asks if I can come in. Two of the waitresses called in sick. You'll have to follow me around with bottles of wine, I say, and he says, you know, you're not as bad as you think you are. You were actually getting pretty good there with the lobsters. He flatters me until I agree and then I immediately wish I hadn't. I locate a tie with crawfish on it, buried underneath my purses in the closet.

Tim thanks me and cups his hand to back of my head. He says, just think about after, when you're counting your money and drinking a cold one. Then he tells me to make some sweet tea and punches me in the arm.

The night goes okay until Rachel, an eleventh grader who rolls her hair, double seats me. One of the tables is a couple and the woman wants to know whether there's butter in this, is there butter in that? I say, I kind of doubt it. She says, could you find out, please? So I go into the kitchen and ask Al if the vegetables are cooked in fat and what about the fish? and he says, just ask her what she wants and we'll do it, which hadn't occurred to me. I say, yeah, good idea, and he laughs good-naturedly, a big sweaty man. I walk back out to the table trying to remember the name of that law or theory that says the simplest explanation is always the best, but all I can come up with is Murphy's Law.

Billy takes forever with a Cape Cod and a beer, and I'm late putting in the appetizer orders. People need drink refills and steak sauce and more bread. And then everyone wants dessert, even the no butter lady orders Key lime pie. Once you get behind, you stay behind, you can't catch up. This is called the weeds and you tell everyone you are in them but no one cares.

I clear seventy dollars, which is bad, which is actually pretty good for me.

At the bar, after everyone's gone, Tim says, you didn't spill anything and no one walked out, so it was a good night. I wrap my hand around his bicep. He flexes. Then he says, come on. Let's get out of here, and I follow him out to his Jeep. I'm not taking you to church tomorrow, I say, and he says, no, please don't. Then he says, I'm sorry about that, and I tell him there's nothing to apologize for. It's already forgotten.

He has a house like the one on my bracelet. I show it to him. He says, a charm bracelet. How charming. I gave my niece one of those for her birthday about a decade ago. He opens a couple of beers and we drink them in his kitchen. I sit on the counter and kick my legs and he just stands there and then he goes to the fridge and takes out a brick of cheese and a couple of apples. Snacks, he says, when he sees me watching him. I eat a hunk of pepper jack; ask if he has any cheddar. It seems like I've done this before, with a hundred other people in a hundred other kitchens.

Where'd you get it? he asks, fingering the saxophone. This guy in my class gave it to me, I say. His name is Norbert. What kind of name is *Norbert*? he says. I shrug. But if you picture a guy named Norbert he probably looks exactly like that.

He stands in between my legs and I tug on his earlobes. Your earlobes are attached. I think that's a dominant trait, I say. I've got hangers, see? Unattached. I push my hair back and look to my right and then my left so he can take a look. Then I tell him that if we have a baby and the baby turns up with brown eyes, he shouldn't pay child support because the kid wouldn't actually be his. He says, so this is what it's like to be inside your head, and I smile and say, it's good in here, which I'm pretty sure is a line from *Being John Malkovich*.

In his bedroom, he opens a dresser and pulls out a t-shirt. Is this okay? he asks, and I nod and undress without turning my back or waiting for him to leave. I brush my teeth with my finger and he brushes his with his toothbrush and we get in bed, lie on our backs. I tell him I'm kind of drunk but it's no excuse. No excuse for what? he asks. We're going to sleep, I say, we're sleeping, and he says okay and then I tell him I just don't want it to be like last time and he says, I've never felt this way before, and I say, what are you talking about? and he says, I'm talking about *you*.

I flip over on my stomach and look at him. He's staring straight up at the ceiling, at a crack in the shape of a loaf of bread. Aw, you like me, I say. How cute. He tells me to shut up and then he puts his hands on my head, threads his fingers through my hair. I lay my head on his chest and breathe, and then I fall asleep, and then I wake up, and then I fall back to sleep and don't wake up until the morning.

We should go to breakfast, he says.

I'm not going anywhere looking like this, I say. I sit up and rake my fingers through my hair.

He takes me to my car and follows me to my apartment, and I shower while he makes coffee. When I come out, I drop my towel and ask if breakfast can wait and then I tell him that the word breakfast comes from the root words break and fast, as in breaking the night's fast with the first meal of the day, and he says he already knew that. You're not going to act weird after, are you? I ask, and he says, no. I'm not going to act weird after. I pull off his shirt. I know how this goes, the undressing, what goes where. I want him to stop me from making the same moves on him that I've made on countless others but he wouldn't recognize them. When we hooked up before, I was driving. I told him I was wet and he said, let me see, and then he got me off while we were stopped at a stop light and an old couple witnessed the entire thing and then he told me they were his grandparents. I thought we were going to be in love after that but he didn't talk to me for a month other than to tell me to make tea or I just got sat or something.

Some people don't like pleasure, he tells me later, over omelets. You're talking about me, I say, and he says, yeah. The boyfriend who moved out West to find himself said something similar. He said I was a machine, that if he ripped me open I'd look like the inside of a wall, but then he was the one who traveled thousands of miles to find something that wasn't lost, so I couldn't believe anything he said. I like pleasure, I say. I've just developed this whole detachment thing because I've been protecting myself for so long. I watch my hands pretend they're birds and then I take a sip of my coffee, and he takes a sip of his and we're sort of pleased with ourselves, with what feels like a revelation but isn't.

ACKNOWLEDGMENTS

This book wouldn't exist without the help, support, and encouragement of the following people:

Elizabeth Ellen, Aaron Burch, Matt Baker, Carol Ann Fitzgerald, Marc Smirnoff, Kim Chinquee, Rick Barthelme, Robert J. Bradley, Jeff Landon, Dave Clapper, David Lindsay, Kathy Pories, Jennifer Pieroni, Adam Pieroni, and Jane Metcalfe Collins.

ABOUT THE AUTHOR

Mary Miller's stories have been published in dozens of print and online journals, including *Black Clock, Mississippi Review, McSweeney's Quarterly, Oxford American, Quick Fiction, elimae, Smokelong Quarterly*, and *Hobart*. Her story "Leak" was selected by ZZ Packer for inclusion in *New Stories from the South, 2008*.